James D

THE
GENESIS
CONSPIRACY

Dedication

To Arthur C. Clark and Michael Crichton for filling my head with what my brother Ben once called "silly stories that only waste time". And to Ben, for being wrong.

Book Description

The most startling secret in human history is about to be revealed...

Buried deep beneath the ocean's surface lies the world's most important discovery.

A piece of modern technology thousands of years old.

To unlock its origins, archaeologist Dr. Martin Anders and a small team will travel to a distant land shrouded in mystery and surrounded by creatures long believed extinct.

But they aren't alone. An ancient order is close behind. And they're determined to suppress a power they believe man was never meant to possess.

The stakes for the human race couldn't be higher. What awaits Anders might not only answer one of man's oldest questions, it could save him from extinction.

The men of Atlantis had subjected the parts of Libya within the columns of Hercules as far as Egypt…
afterwards there occurred violent earthquakes and floods; and in a single day… the island of Atlantis… disappeared in the depths of the sea.

PLATO

Chapter 1

Pyrenees Mountains, Spain
August 1, 2059

Archaeologist Juan Garcia removed his oxygen mask and glared up at the largest glacier in the Pyrenees. "We're nearly there," he said to his colleague, Marcelino Heras. Both men were buzzing with excitement. And for good reason. Entombed in the ice somewhere up there was a discovery that could rewrite history.

Twenty-four hours ago, a group of Austrian mountain climbers stumbled upon a discolored rock poking up from the ice. When one of them chipped at it with his ice pick, they discovered that it wasn't a rock at all. It was the back of a human skull.

They contacted the local authorities and a forensics team was sent to investigate. After clearing some of the snow, the police quickly realized this was no lost climber.

Their call to the local university was intercepted by a testy receptionist who transferred the cops to the department of archeology and anthropology.

That was when Juan had answered.

And now here they were, but Juan knew that eagerness was one thing, and getting to the body in one piece was another. The problem was rather simple; the glacier atop Mount Aneto was melting, every day becoming more unstable.

In nineteen eighty-four, a survey of the glacier had measured the ice pack at nearly a dozen miles long. Since then, eighty percent of it had been lost. Within a decade, the mountain would be bare. A reality which made the team's trek to the summit that much more important and that much more difficult.

With this in mind, Juan and Marcelino charged on, forcing one leg in front of the other. Slowly they made progress as they struggled to haul heavy backpacks loaded with equipment up the mountain's eleven thousand feet.

Two hours later, they finally found what they were looking for. The authorities had been wise enough to leave a triangle of evidence flags to mark the location. Dropping their packs nearby, Juan and Marcelino got to work at once.

The process of digging through ice compacted over several millennia was slow. But soon enough, the glacier began to reveal its secrets.

First to become visible was an upper torso with flesh the color of rich amber. Assigning an accurate date to the body while on-site would be difficult. They would need contextual—items such as a Bronze Age ax, a quiver of arrows, or if they were exceptionally lucky a few scraps of clothing. Regardless, the state of the body made one thing perfectly clear: whoever this person once was, they had remained trapped in the ice for many thousands of years.

Marcelino was digging under the body to free the legs when he stopped and let out a quiet little sigh.

"You find something?" Juan asked, glancing up from his analysis of the skull.

"Yes, but I don't see how it can be."

Juan stood and came around, his feet crunching over the dense ice sheet.

"Reach your hand inside the hole I dug," Marcelino instructed him. "Tell me what you feel."

Juan removed his glove, wiggling his fingers against the cold. He reached in, at first touching snow, then the smooth, marble-like flesh of the body before he felt it. His eyes narrowed with confusion then grew wide with shock.

"Is this what I think it is?" he whispered under his breath.

Marcelino's head bobbed up and down. "Impossible, I know, and yet there it is."

Juan removed a small flashlight from his pocket and peered into the gap. Diamonds of light danced over an object that shouldn't be present on a body this old.

It looked like a zipper.

•••

After the archaeologists finally freed the body, it was flown to the quaint Pyrenees village of Sallent de Gallego, where the university housed one of its satellite research facilities.

There, the body was kept in a nitrogen-rich atmospheric chamber with a relative humidity of ninety-

3

eight percent. The initial temperature was set to minus six Celsius, but was gradually warmed to allow the ice crystals to melt.

Before long, they discovered that the individual in question—affectionately named Johnny Doe—was a middle-aged male. Isotopic analysis of the teeth showed he had lived in North Africa, but it was the carbon-14 dating that really surprised them. Juan had already figured out the body was old, going back as many as five thousand years, but when Marcelino read the date, Juan could hardly believe it.

"Twelve thousand years," Juan yelped.

He paused, struggling to slow his breathing. Johnny Doe was more than twice as old and far better preserved than any previous find in the history of archaeology. But Juan's euphoria was tempered by the strange discovery that had accompanied him: the remnants of what could only be described as a zipper running the length of the body.

"Could it somehow have been placed there afterward?" he wondered outloud. He needed to find a solution that made sense or the archaeological community would tear him apart.

"There was a small amount of fabric attached to the zipper line," Marcelino told him. "It appears to be a synthetic material, rubberized plastic perhaps. If I had to guess I'd say it was a body bag."

Juan's gaze, deep and penetrating, flicked over in his direction. They had been in this room for nearly two days straight and Juan's head was swimming. Since lunch his heart had been galloping in his chest, his flesh rosy and warm to the touch. Signs he'd associated with being overworked and underfed.

Marcelino was in the middle of proposing a fresh hypothesis about their puzzling zipper discovery when a stream of blood rolled out from his left nostril.

Juan watched it pass over his friend's lip and down his chin. He pointed, waving his finger, unable to quite get the words out. Then came another stream, this one from Marcelino's other nostril. His friend and colleague wiped it away with the back of his hand, staring down at the crimson smear.

Something was terribly wrong.

Juan turned to leave the chamber when Marcelino collapsed, his head hitting the floor with a wet slap. He rushed for a phone, to call an ambulance for the man who'd become like a brother to him.

Juan stopped before the glass door. The phone was on the other side. His numb fingers fumbled over the keypad. The code was simple, the same four digits he'd entered probably a thousand times before, but for some reason he couldn't remember them at all. Panic surged into his throat as he tried again, the final digit followed by an angry buzz and the glare of a red light.

Denied.

He glanced up, terror clawing at his every breath. Raising an arm to hammer the glass with a closed fist, Juan caught his own reflection in the glass door. Thick streams of blood ran from his nose, ears and eyes.

Suddenly his dreams of becoming a celebrated academic seemed a million miles away. His eyes flickered back toward the ancient body thawing on the gurney, and a final thought had time to slither through his infected mind as he wondered what horror they had just unleashed?

Chapter 2

Prague, Czech Republic
August 15, 2059 (Two Weeks Later)

The assassin arrived just as the street lamps flickered on, the light casting long, winding shadows over the faces of the gothic buildings along Celetna Street. The humidity in Prague this time of year was thick and hung about the cast-iron lanterns in a heavy mist. He drew in a lungful of damp air and then spat onto the cobblestone sidewalk. You could nearly taste the Vltava River.

The sound of approaching footsteps was followed by a blur of movement as the assassin melted into a web of shadow nearby. A moment later, a young couple emerged, stumbling down the narrow street, giggling at each other in Czech, their voices echoing off the facades of the old apartments. They appeared to be in love, perhaps on their way home from a romantic dinner. A single strap from the woman's fine dress dangled off her left shoulder. The man, stylish and handsome, a regular Casanova, eyed her longingly. They stopped long enough for Casanova to take her by the shoulders and ease her against the wall. He began to kiss her passionately, the woman moaning with delight, whispering to her lover not to stop.

From out of the inky blackness the assassin lit the tip of a cigarette, the flame illuminating a pair of soulless eyes. Even in the dim light it was clear these were the eyes of a killer.

"Get lost!" the assassin whispered in broken Czech.

Startled, the woman squealed with fright. Casanova took a step back, his perfect hair disheveled, his mouth open like a fish plucked from an aquarium.

Without needing to be told twice, the man broke into a run, followed closely by his lover.

Soon the nighttime calm was back and the assassin returned to his vigil, a dull ember glowing from his lips. As streets went in Prague, Celetna was like any other: long and crooked and normally thronged with daytime tourists wearing khaki shorts and fanny packs, licking at soggy ice cream cones and headed for the Powder Tower or the old Jewish Cemetery or the Tyn Cathedral. But the sun had long since disappeared, and so too had they, back to the safety of their hotel rooms, back to their television sets and fat paperback novels and plump wives who probably couldn't remember the last time they'd known anything like real happiness.

Then at last he saw what he'd been waiting for: a shadow brushing past the curtain in the apartment above him. The target was home. That was the good news. Even better was the open window. It wasn't open much more than a crack, but a crack was all he needed.

He reached for the tiny metal case in his pocket, exposing the tattoo on his forearm—five small circles that formed a cross. A symbol that embodied the very reason he was here. He flipped open the lid and examined the contents inside.

For all intents and purposes the device looked like an insect, had been designed that way. Small and rounded, its bumblebee body bristled with microscopic hairs, its delicate wings folded inside themselves. As the lid had come open, so too had its eyes, glowing now blood red in the damp night air like two living rubies. He let the cigarette tumble from his fingers and crushed it with the ball of his foot.

There was a light on in the room upstairs, the one with the cracked window. In the assassin's free hand was a remote. He pushed and held the button and the insect's thin wings unfurled and began to flap. It lifted off and danced across weak currents of air. Rising and falling, flowing left and right. Up it flew, struggling past the iron lantern, past the red awning outside a shop that pawned cheap goods to naïve tourists. At last, the insect's spindly legs scrambled onto the window frame and it waddled into the room, undetected.

On a table next to a plush velvet couch sat an antique lamp with a shade the color of rough diamond. The insect took to the air again, lumbered slowly, drunkenly across the room and landed on the shade.

The assassin watched all this from the street below on a digital wristwatch. Upstairs, the insect scanned the room before locating the target.

Dr. Gustave Hiddenger was an older man with a swollen belly, stuffed into a pair of khaki shorts, his legs white and pasty.

The doctor licked his lips as he shoved clothing into a duffel bag. His arms were short and hairy. His undershirt, gray with dirt and perspiration, clung to his back and sides. No doubt about it, the fat man was afraid and he had every reason to be.

A manila envelope sat on the bed nearby, papers strewn around it. The letterhead showed a crescent moon curled around a double helix.

"Genesis," the assassin whispered knowingly before he pressed a button on his watch and began heading south on Celetna Street. That was about the time Dr. Hiddenger spotted the fly with the glowing red eyes. On his face, the twitching expression slowly morphed from confusion to terror. The insect's eyes were blinking now, blinking away the seconds, counting down the time until the man would be no more.

The assassin turned the corner just as Celetna Street was illuminated by a bright, thundering light and an ear-shattering explosion. The buildings around him shook to their very foundations. The windows blew out, the glass tumbling to the ground like sparkling jewels. It would only be the following day that the authorities would find Hiddenger's head, lodged between the cushions in an apartment across the street, that terrified recognition of death still plastered on the remains of his broken face.

Chapter 3

The Following Day
Location: 400 nautical miles off the coast of Portugal

A single white dot bobbed in a vast expanse of ocean. The former fishing trawler-turned-research vessel was old and in desperate need of repairs. Peeled lettering on the stern spelled out the ship's name: *Lady Luck*.

Along the aft deck, three figures were busy at work. One was manning the winch that fed an air hose to the atmospheric diving suit currently a thousand feet beneath them. Another was using a joystick to operate the ROUV (remotely operated underwater vehicle). While the third sat a few feet away, using a toothbrush to scrub hundreds and in some cases thousands of years of concretion from archaeological artifacts.

Inside the wheelhouse, Dr. Martin Anders was asleep in his captain's chair, his feet propped up on the console.

Resting in his lap was a foldable digital newspaper with a headline that read:

CDC Warns: Mysterious Flu Spreads at Alarming Rate.

Before him sat rows of high-tech equipment. One bank of monitors showed the grainy images of the diver beneath them, lumbering around in his bulky suit. Above that, more screens displayed activity on the deck. To the right, a third set of readouts showed the diver's current biometrics.

Soon the diver in the heavy suit turned to the camera and began waving his arms.

"Chief, you there?" His excited voice sounded distorted and otherworldly.

The slumbering Anders didn't respond. Didn't even stir.

The diver adjusted a setting in his helmet and called again, this time so loudly it nearly shattered the wheelhouse windows.

Anders jolted awake with a start, knocking an open bottle of Jack Daniels onto the floor. He swore and scooped up the newspaper now resting at his feet and flung it across the room. Next to leave the floor was the bottle of booze, but rather than launching it, Anders screwed the cap back on, lamenting the wasted puddle at his feet, and set it on the chart table.

That was when he spotted the brown paper parcel. The box was no bigger than a few inches squared, but it hadn't been there when he'd closed his eyes earlier for a quick nap.

"Wake up, Chief," came the diver's booming voice again.

Annoyed, Anders fingered the comm switch. "What is it, Sykes? I was in the middle of something important."

"You're not gonna believe what I just found."

"This better not be another Coke bottle."

11

"Preparing to send it topside now," Sykes replied, already opening a carabiner and connecting the pouch to an airbag. "Won't be long."

Anders exited the wheelhouse into a burst of blinding sunlight, tucking the small brown paper package under his arm as he paused to rub the sleep out of his eyes. With a full head of wavy brown hair and a face covered with stubble, Anders might have recently celebrated his thirty-fifth birthday, but he could easily have passed for a man ten years his senior. One of his female PhD students, a stocky twenty-something named Rodriguez, often said there was an incredibly handsome man hiding under all that scruff just waiting to be uncovered. Much like the artifacts they drudged up from the ocean floor.

Speaking of artifacts, on deck, Rodriguez had her arms elbow deep in a plastic bin, rubbing at thick layers of grime from a recent discovery. She tilted her head and noticed the package Anders had started to examine.

"Came in by float plane while you were asle—" She stopped herself. "Uh, I mean, busy. Birthday present from your mother."

Anders tossed it onto a table covered with nautical charts and underwater camera equipment.

"Aren't you going to open it?" she asked, incredulous.

"Why bother? She sends me the same thing every year, a black leather wallet. I got a collection of empty ones in the wheelhouse if you're interested."

Rodriguez grinned, but the implication of Anders' comment was clear enough. "Don't worry. The funding will come through. I can feel it."

Anders squeezed her shoulder as he moved past.

Over by the stern, Binh Nguyen, his second mate and best bud, waited for the lifting bags to break the surface. Small and weathered, his Vietnamese friend sported a mouthful of bad teeth and an attitude to match. Binh's three main pleasures in life were chain-smoking, drinking and gambling. But his eyes really lit up on those rare occasions when he managed to combine all three vices in a single medley of self-destruction.

A cigarette with an impossibly long ash dangled from Binh's lips as he said something cutting to Anders in Boatese. A language that few outsiders understood, Boatese was a garbled Asiatic dialogue spoken by an ethnic mix of boat people. It was a name given by developed countries to refugees displaced from coastal regions by melting ice and rising tides. By some estimates, they made up over fifty percent of the current global population. Not surprisingly, their arrival at Western ports had quickly overwhelmed many of the wealthier nations. In an effort to solve the problem, outdated container ships had been assembled to house the flood of immigrants. It was supposed to be a temporary measure, but twenty years on, many of the world's ports were still clogged with aging tankers and container ships converted into squalid living platforms. Not surprisingly, boat people were commonly regarded by the more affluent land-based classes as little more than rodents.

Anders said, "I wouldn't complain about not getting paid. Consider yourself lucky you have a job."

Binh shook his head and muttered under his breath.

"Don't you worry your pretty little head," Anders shot back, marveling at how easily Binh could punch his buttons. The two of them were worse than an old married couple. "You'll get paid. You'll all get paid."

Next to Rodriguez and looking decidedly uncomfortable stood Ben Carter, an undergrad with an early receding hairline. As neither of his students spoke Boatese, they were often left to piece together the disagreement from Anders' rebukes.

Few understood that Anders needed Binh more than he liked to admit. Universities didn't see the scholarly merit in chasing after mythology. So when official funding for Anders' fanciful expeditions had dried up, he'd fallen back on Binh's connections to the seedy Boatese underworld to meet his monthly expenses. That rather fateful decision had meant a significant percentage of their finds were now handed over to gangsters and forever swallowed up in the black market for archaeological artifacts. It was a choice that had nearly broken Anders' heart, but his quest had taken him from the depths of the Aegean through the Pillars of Hercules and now into the Atlantic. And he knew it was only a question of time before he found what he was looking for—the lost continent of Atlantis, surely the greatest archaeological discovery of all time.

The sharp sound of thrusters drew Anders' attention.

"Cutter inbound on our starboard side," Carter called out as he tracked the aircraft through a pair of binoculars.

Anders' pulse spiked. It seemed they were about to have company and something told him it wouldn't be the good kind.

Chapter 4

The approaching Cutter was a class of aircraft that might have passed for a military Osprey, minus the oversized rotors. In their place were a pair of thrusters mounted beneath the wings and capable of transitioning to enable hovering as well as forward flight. The underbelly of this particular iteration was also rounded, allowing it to land in water and remain afloat.

Slowly, the craft made its descent, settling into the ocean less than ten yards away. A hatch peeled open and a sailor in a crisp white uniform popped out and fired a rope cannon toward the *Lady Luck*. Carter caught the line and secured it to one of the boat cleats.

"You expecting someone?" Anders asked Binh, who shrugged his shoulders.

Once the Cutter was brought alongside, a late-middle-aged man in a dark suit and a respirator emerged. He had a large pair of fleshy ears and a receding hairline to match. He had no sooner come on deck than the ship pitched slightly and the man stiffened in an attempt to stabilize himself.

Anders could see he was out of his element. The man removed his mask and extended an unsteady hand toward Carter. "Dr. Anders, I presume. My name is Charles Davenport and I'm here on behalf of my employer, Ali Khan, the owner and CEO of Genesis Corporation."

Hesitantly, Carter accepted the open palm, turning slowly to Anders, who was over by the wheelhouse, drying his hands. This wasn't the first time Anders' gruff appearance had caused him to be mistaken for a deckhand. Binh, on the other hand, made no effort to hide the satisfaction he got whenever it happened.

"Genesis, eh?" Anders said, setting the cloth down on a nearby table. "I don't seem to remember lawyers in the Old Testament. Do you, Binh?"

Binh returned a puzzled expression and said he'd never heard of the Old Testament.

Clearly embarrassed, but determined not to show it, Davenport crossed the deck toward Anders. "Is there somewhere we can talk?" he asked.

"I don't keep secrets from my crew, Mr. Davenport. Anything you need to know you ask me right here in the open."

Davenport straightened. "Very well. My employer, Mr. Khan, has come to understand your recent requests for further funding have been denied."

The expressions on Binh's and Rodriguez's faces twisted at once.

"Denied?" she barked. "When were you going to tell us?"

"We also understand, Dr. Anders, that certain interested parties are eager to collect on a list of debts still unpaid. At the top of that list is one Mr. Chiu, a noted underworld figure from the Boatese community."

Anders had been wrong about Davenport. The man wasn't as incompetent as he looked. "I'm not sure where you got your information, Mr. Davenport, but…"

"We also understand that Mr. Chiu has threatened to take possession of this research vessel and separate your head from the rest of your body if he's not paid what he's owed."

"That Chiu's all talk."

Davenport rubbed his palms together. "We'd like to make you an offer. We're putting a team together, a handful of consultants, each of them specialists in their respective fields. Your services wouldn't be required for more than a day. Two at the most. We'd pay you, of course."

Just then the water off the catwalk began to churn, signaling the arrival of the float bag. The yellow canvas inflatable broke the surface and bobbed twice before Binh and Carter broke from the group to wrestle it out of the sea. The object was heavily encrusted and the two men strained under the weight. Anders moved in to help cradle the object and deposit it into a plastic container filled with a protective chemical solution.

"I'm flattered, Mr. Davenport, but as you can see, I'm really too busy for any extra work."

Davenport seemed unfazed. "I've been authorized to offer you fifty thousand up front to come and hear our proposal. Upon acceptance, Genesis Corp is prepared to fully fund your excavations for the next five years. Oh, and as a gratuity, we'll see to it your debts with Mr. Chiu are settled."

Anders crossed his arms. "I've had offers like this before, Mr. Davenport, and they've all ended badly. See, corporations like yours can't help but tinker with the work we do."

17

"Let me assure you there will be no tinkering on our part. You may very well choose to spend the money studying the mating habits of sea cucumbers. It makes no difference to us. Plus, look on the bright side. You get to keep your head."

Anders was torn. With the little money they had left, the expedition might last another week, two at the most. Even then, there weren't enough pilfered artifacts Anders could put into Chiu's grimy hands to offset the high-interest loans he'd been forced to take. His life wasn't the only one on the line. Chiu's loan-sharking minions had only entertained Anders' request after Binh had called in favors from the community. If that money wasn't repaid, Anders wouldn't be the only one with a severed head.

"I think you better take a look at this," Carter said from the stern of the ship. He was kneeling down over the object they'd just fished out of the sea.

Chapter 5

In three strides, Anders left a rather bewildered Davenport to see what Carter had found. Protruding from the coral mass Sykes had sent up was a horribly mangled metal plate. The amount of coral made it plain to see the object it encased was exceptionally old, but even at first glance, the metal had clearly been fabricated using modern metallurgical processes.

"No rust or corrosion?" Rodriguez observed, dumbfounded.

"Get a radiometric reading on that coral, would you?" Anders told her. "And see if we can figure out how long it's been down there."

Moments later, Rodriguez returned with a spectrometer: a handheld device they would use to count the carbon-14 atoms in the sample to provide them with an approximate date the coral had formed.

Rodriguez depressed a switch, releasing a tiny drill head which began spinning. Pushing the blade against the surface, Rodriguez burrowed into the coral block until the light turned green.

"We should have an answer in a few minutes," she said.

But of course, Anders wasn't going to just wait around. Pushing past Davenport, he fetched an X-ray wand and waved it over the object. The device would scan through the coral to get a better look at the metal trapped inside. The X-rayed image appeared on a small flickering screen next to them.

Anders perched a clipboard over the display to block out the sun. His pulse quickened as the image slowly came into focus. At first, he saw nothing but a series of strange symbols etched on the surface.

Perched over his shoulder, Carter said, "I'll admit it's been a while since high school, but some of that looks a heck of a lot like trigonometry to me. That one with the squiggly line…"

"The sign for pi," Anders said, slowly, deliberately, intent on containing his excitement. Jumping to conclusions now wouldn't be prudent, no matter how much he wanted to do exactly that. "And this one here," Anders continued, running his finger over the faint image. "Instructions for harvesting grain. Looks like one of Mivers' cheat sheets."

"One of what?" Davenport asked, clearly caught up in the excitement and eager to get up to speed.

Anders used the tips of his fingers to swipe the X-ray off the screen and called up a fuzzy image similar to what they'd seen on the metal plate. "Twenty years ago a French archaeologist named Jules Mivers captured this image using ground-penetrating radar a few yards from the Sphinx."

"The one in Egypt?" Davenport wondered out loud.

Anders stared at him. "You know any other Sphinx?"

Davenport shook his head.

"Mivers believed that all cultures shared a common origin. And that if you could go back far enough, you would find the first civilization that gave birth to those that followed."

"And what do you suppose that might look like?" Davenport asked.

"Through myth we've come to know it as the lost continent of Atlantis," Anders said.

"You believe this plate is connected somehow?"

"We do," Anders replied.

Davenport's face clouded with confusion. "You'd think a discovery on that scale would have been a major find. Wouldn't Mivers have published in a peer-reviewed journal somewhere?"

Anders grinned. "Mivers submitted to a dozen journals and was soundly rejected by each and every one. You see, there's a vague line between academics and politics. To cross that line is to find your work swallowed in a black hole of obscurity. For some folks, the very idea that ancient cultures like those in Egypt and Mesopotamia were seeded by a much older and far more sophisticated civilization is far too threatening. For others, it's tantamount to sacrilege."

"Then you're saying there was a conspiracy to silence him," Davenport suggested, his crossed arms crumpling the edges of his suit.

"I'm saying that twelve thousand years ago, farming, animal domestication, irrigation, and the first inklings of civilization and technology seem to have sprung up out of nowhere and nobody really knows why. Textbooks call it the Neolithic Revolution, but it should really be called the Mysterious Leap Forward.

Next to him, Rodriguez had goosebumps on her arms in spite of the noonday sun bearing down on them.

"What I'm saying is whoever made this plate would have made the ancient Egyptians look like a mob of knuckle-dragging cavemen."

Chapter 6

They stood silently on the deck of the *Lady Luck*, each of them considering what Anders had just said. The spell was shattered by the squeal of the spectrometer.

"Date's in on the coral," Rodriguez announced, glancing down at the device. The breath hitched in her throat. "You're not gonna believe this."

The look on Anders' face said, *Try me.*

Rodriguez made a quick mental calculation. "The plate's clocking in at twelve thousand years old."

"Are you sure?" Anders said, running his fingers through the thick crop of hair on his head.

"10,423 BCE, plus or minus twenty years," she replied.

Davenport seemed astonished and a touch uneasy.

Anders shook his head. "Run it again."

Rodriguez sighed. "I'm also picking up radiation levels that are above background. Not enough to be dangerous, but they're there."

"This keeps getting better," Anders said. "Let me know when you've run those dates again."

Rodriguez was in the process of taking another sample when a second float bag broke the surface. Binh scooped it out on his own, depositing what looked like a coral softball into a fresh bucket. Anders swooped in with the X-ray wand. After a quick pass he swiveled to study the image populating on the display screen.

He zeroed in on what looked like a series of monochrome cogs and wheels.

"Center screen and adjust contrast," Anders ordered the computer.

Gears of varying sizes came into focus.

"Think it's another Antikythera mechanism?" Rodriguez asked, open-mouthed.

She was referring to the nineteenth-century discovery of what some had called the first computer. Named after the island where the object was found, the two-thousand-year-old Antikythera mechanism was a clockwork of gears and cogs, designed, among other things, to calculate astronomical positions.

Anders shook his head. "It's far too small." He paused to rub the scruff on his chin.

"Forgive my ignorance," Davenport said, leaning in. "But I'd be tempted to say it looks like a wrist watch."

The comment drew a noticeable reaction. Ignoring the gasps as well as the sweltering heat, Anders charged on. "Go to ultraviolet."

The computer complied.

"Magnify." A second later. "Stop."

"Are those…?" Carter began.

"Letters, yes," Anders said. "An engraving." He read them out. "I… N… D… W… H…" But the rest was illegible.

Rodriguez squealed. "Letters from a modern English alphabet. That's not possible."

"Print copy," Anders commanded the computer. The display began whirring before a snapshot emerged from a hidden slot beneath the screen.

Beside him, Rodriguez studied the readout from the spectrometer.

"Dates from the object are in the same range as the plate."

Anders dropped to one knee, reached into the bucket and ran the tips of his fingers over the rough edges of the coral concretion. None of this was what they'd expected to find. A titanium plate with strange inscriptions along with what seemed to be a watch, both seeming to date back over twelve thousand years. But difficult as it was to believe, the data didn't lie.

Binh dropped down beside him and spoke in Boatese. He wanted to know what Anders made of all this.

Anders shook the briny solution from his hand. "Whatever is going on here, it's big." His hand dropped to his pocket and the picture of their mysterious new discovery.

Davenport stood nearby, waiting patiently for Anders' answer.

Drawing in a deep breath, Anders couldn't shake the skittish feeling he was about to make a terrible mistake. "All right, I'll come and listen to your pitch," he said. "But on one condition."

Sensing victory, Davenport barely fought the grin forming on his narrow lips. "Name it."

"Binh comes too."

For a moment, Davenport appeared surprised, maybe even stunned. He looked up and down Binh's slender frame, appearing decidedly unimpressed. "As you wish."

And with that, Binh broke into a proud smile, his mouth a patchwork of brown, crooked teeth.

The two men quickly threw a few belongings together and headed for the Cutter. Rodriguez called out as they made ready to climb onboard. Anders turned in time to see an object sailing through the air toward him. He reached out and caught the package, grinning when he saw what she'd thrown him: the present from his mother.

"She'd kill me if she knew you'd left it behind."

Anders gave them a final look before he pulled the hatch closed.

Chapter 7

The Cutter jostled in strong winds as the plane approached the coast of Portugal. Soon after that, Lisbon came into view, its port crammed with docked cargo ships of all sizes. This was only one of the hundreds of coastal cities the boat people called home. Their presence made the area look far more like the congested waters of the nineteenth century than anything belonging to the mid-twenty-first. Over the last fifty years the city had ballooned as a result of runaway population growth, stretching now like a fungus for miles and miles.

From that ungainly sight, the Cutter banked right and headed south. Anders was surprised since he had assumed they'd be heading inland.

He removed the gift from his mother and studied the brown paper she'd used to wrap it. She'd never understood his passion for unearthing relics from lost civilizations. If he'd given in to her incessant demands, Anders might have become a banker or a lawyer. No doubt about it, the money would have been better, but his soul would have shriveled to the size of a peach pit. Not everyone was built to sit behind a desk and take orders.

Anders had been forced to find his inspiration far from home. After he'd received his PhD in maritime archaeology from the University of Cape Town, South Africa, his mentor, the reclusive Dr. Gustave Hiddenger, had laid out an impressive case for the possible location of the fabled island of Atlantis. At the beginning, the two discussed the subject as a lark. Whenever Anders expressed doubt in its existence, his professor would invoke the ghost of Heinrich Schliemann, the nineteenth-century German businessman who had suffered endless ridicule for his use of Homer's *The Iliad* as a primary source in his search for the lost city of Troy. Despite Schliemann's questionable methods, his eventual success had been a source of joy for the man and an embarrassment for the supposedly learned academics who had doubted him.

Much like Schliemann, Hiddenger had turned to Plato's Socratic dialogue *Timaeus* as a starting point for his own search. In one short section, Critias had described Solon, the great lawgiver, meeting with a group of Egyptian priests where he was told of Atlantis.

According to Plato, Atlantis was a powerful island nation whose capital city was said to be a series of concentric rings, each thicker than the last. Over the years the men of Atlantis had sought to enslave those living nearby until a violent cataclysm destroyed them and all of their ambitions in a single day.

If the advanced seagoing civilization Plato described was more than just a myth, the most likely candidate was the Greek island of Santorini. At least, that was how Hiddenger saw it. The volcanic eruption which had devastated Santorini in 1600BC certainly made it an interesting candidate, not to mention the similarities in soil makeup as outlined by Plato. Despite several exhaustive explorations in and around the island, any concrete link with Atlantis continued to elude them. The ridicule they received from colleagues, however, was always plentiful. In no time, they had learned a difficult lesson that in the academic world, few subjects were more deadly to one's professional career. And it hadn't been long before the snickers led to money troubles. Within a year, the funding had dried up and Hiddenger had been forced into retirement, a broken and bitter man.

A tap on his shoulder yanked Anders from his thoughts. Beside him, Binh was pointing out the window toward a magnificent sight. The sky was streaked with bands of red, orange and yellow as the sun slowly slipped from view. Anders found himself grinning at the sight, eager to replace the memory of Hiddenger's disgrace. But that wasn't what Binh wanted him to see. His Vietnamese friend motioned again, this time down toward the cobalt-blue ocean beneath them. Anders leaned in and his jaw went slack.

In the distance and growing larger by the second was Genesis' majestic research ship, the *Excelsior*. Sleek and gleaming white, it looked like something out of Greek mythology. Anders pressed his face up against the glass like a kid peering through a toy store window, a single envious desire settling on his lips.

"I want one," he said.

Chapter 8

The glowing red H on the helipad grew larger as the Cutter settled over it and prepared to land. Four retractable wheels emerged from the hull and locked into place. Below them, deckhands in white uniforms used marshaling wands to guide the pilot's descent. The aircraft shook slightly as it touched down.

Anders and Binh popped their seatbelts off and attempted to stretch their legs in the cramped confines of the cabin. Outside, a crew member pulled open the door, revealing a set of stairs.

Davenport appeared on the landing pad, struggling to flatten the wrinkles in his expensive dress pants. He straightened and smiled. "Welcome to the *Excelsior*, gentlemen."

They followed Davenport through a watertight hatch. A striking woman in a gray suit awaited them inside. Flanking her were two Genesis security personnel in blue.

"I trust both of you had a pleasant flight," she said, extending her hand, which was pale and delicate. She was somewhere in her late twenties, her auburn hair tied up in a ponytail, her figure athletic. "I'm Ms. Meadows, personal assistant to Mr. Khan."

Davenport shuddered ever so slightly as she spoke. A subtle move, but one Anders caught nevertheless. From little more than a glance, he could tell these two didn't get along. Hard to believe anyone having trouble getting along with a woman with her looks. It pointed to professional tensions. Perhaps Meadows had beat the old man out for a job. Either way, the sight left Anders with an uneasy feeling. They'd barely set foot off the Cutter and already signs of trouble in paradise were becoming apparent.

"You may want to freshen up before your meeting with Mr. Khan," Meadows offered. "We have a fully equipped spa on deck five. Otherwise, I can show you to your quarters."

Binh made a crude comment.

She fixed him with a cold stare. "I'm sorry, I missed that. What did he say?"

Anders shook his head. "Trust me, you don't wanna know."

When she was gone, Anders grabbed Binh by the shoulder and spun him around. "I'm gonna need you on your best behavior," he told him. "We're onto something big back at the excavation site. Which means from here on the expedition will only get more expensive. I don't need to be the one to tell you that the money from this gig could help save our asses. What I'm saying is don't go messing this up."

Binh shook his head, feigning indignation.

But Anders wasn't buying it for a second. "And for God's sake, promise me this time you won't steal anything."

•••

Thirty minutes later, clean-cut and freshly shaven, Anders and Binh made their way to the boardroom. A pair of doors swished open as they arrived. The room inside was cool and lavishly decorated. In the center was a table made from extinct cherrywood trees. On the far wall hung an enormous central screen flanked on either side by three-dimensional monitors. As they entered, a well-dressed female hologram silently beckoned them to take a seat. Binh stopped, looking amazed as he ran his hand through the image.

That was when Anders realized they weren't the first to arrive. Two men and a woman were already seated, and Anders recognized each of them immediately.

"I had a feeling this was too good to be true," Dr. Anita Riese said, without trying to hide her disdain. She was fierce and attractive, with a degree in molecular virology from Harvard Medical. She was a renowned perfectionist and control freak. Her striking blue eyes followed them coolly as they entered.

The two of them had met at a conference in Brussels on the reemergence of long-dormant diseases released by the melting permafrost. They'd shared a few drinks and then she'd shared Anders' bed. That was the last time they'd spoken.

Seated next to her was Dr. Ivan Khazanov, an archaeology and linguistics whiz from St Petersburg. Built like a bear, he was best known for his booming laugh and love of hard alcohol.

Last and most certainly least was Dr. Daniel Erwin. The bespectacled paleobotanist was a man who probably couldn't get a date even if he paid for it.

"Lookie-lookie what the cat dragged in," Erwin said, sneering. He was as thin as he was arrogant.

Anders planted his feet and smiled. "Ernie, they invite you too? I was sure Oxford had you locked in the botany wing counting tree rings from the Pleistocene."

Khazanov clapped his hands together with a deafening echo. "Hey, even plant stiffs need to piss in the wind from time to time, no?"

"Very funny. Very funny. For your information I've been busy publishing papers."

"Papers," Anders replied, scanning the ceiling as though trying to recall. "No, never heard of 'em."

Erwin shook his head and crossed his arms. "I'm sure you haven't."

To his left, Riese let out a quiet laugh. "I read your work on Neolithic trade routes, Dr. Anders."

"So did I," Erwin cut in obnoxiously, "and I have to say your methodology was weak. Frankly, I'm not sure how you keep getting funding."

Anders locked eyes with Riese. "What did you think?"

"I think you never called back," she said, clearly talking about something else.

"Watch out, Anders," Khazanov warned him. "This one bites."

Riese folded her arms.

Anders smiled weakly. Binh gave Riese a thumbs up. She grinned, doing her best to avoid Anders' gaze.

"She's no shrinking violet," Khazanov said, rubbing the table's fine finish. "I heard the professor of microbiology who was mentoring Dr. Riese's PhD found that out the hard way. Word around town was he started getting… frisky. Isn't that right, Anita? I heard you knocked his front tooth out." Khazanov could barely finish before his large frame began gyrating with laughter.

"You heard wrong, Ivan," Riese corrected him. "I've never hit a man in my life. All I did was swing my knee

33

between his legs. Funny, his nubby hands never did wander again after that." She paused to reminisce.

Just then the conference doors swung open and in strode Ali Khan, the director of Genesis Corp, flanked by Meadows and Davenport. Anders and Binh settled into their seats as Khan and the others stopped to face them. In the background, the display screens flickered to life with the company's logo: an azure-blue crescent moon centered with a red double helix.

"Ladies and gentlemen," Khan said, his voice betraying the hint of an Indian accent. "You'll have to forgive me if we forgo the usual formalities. By now I'm sure each of you is wondering who I am and why I've brought you together."

"You were an environmentalist," Erwin blurted out, always the teacher's pet. "When your father passed away, your mother begged you to take over the family's steel business. Reluctantly you agreed and in the span of a decade you grew the company into an international powerhouse. Since then, Genesis has scooped up companies in the transportation as well as biomedical fields." Erwin's cheeks reddened. "I looked you up on the internet."

A grin spread over Khan's aging features. Something about his salt-and-pepper hair and the way he squared his shoulders lent him an undeniable air of authority. "I see you've done your homework, Dr. Erwin. But allow me to get straight to the point and explain why I brought you here. Three weeks ago, climbers hiking in the Pyrenees discovered a body frozen in the ice. Even to their untrained eye, it was clear they were dealing with something very, very old."

"I saw a piece on the news about it not long ago," Riese said, reclining in her plush chair. "They thought it might be older than Otzi."

34

The Otzi Iceman was a five-thousand-year-old male whose frozen remains had been discovered by mountain climbers in 1991. He had been almost perfectly preserved, down to the tools lying next to him and the tattoos that marked his flesh.

"Yes, but I can't say I've heard anything since," Khazanov added. "Sounded to me as though it were the find of a lifetime. You can imagine we've all been anxious to learn more."

Khan rubbed his hands together and then stopped. "I'm afraid there was a very good reason for the silence. Shortly after the body was removed from the mountain, it was brought to the village of Sallent de Gallego and carefully thawed for study. During that process, something happened."

"Happened?" Anders repeated, a hint of concern in his voice.

"Apparently the trapped odor of decomposing flesh wasn't the only thing that escaped during the thawing," Khan said.

Erwin straightened his back. "They released a virus, didn't they?"

"Yes, and an incredibly dangerous one at that."

"Pyrenean hemorrhagic fever or PHF," Riese told them, her voice registering fear. "Some are calling it the new Spanish flu, others the red death because of the way the infected's blood oozes from every orifice. Except, unlike the Spanish flu, this one's spreading much, much faster."

Anders was still digesting the bit where the disease had come from a thawing body dead thousands of years. This sort of thing had been the very subject of the conference he and Riese had attended. "How old a bug are we talking about here?" he asked.

"Ancient..." Khan started to say.

"Is that even possible?" Khazanov cut in, amazed. "I mean, could it really survive that long?"

"Longer," Riese informed him. "A thirty-thousand-year-old bug was dug up from the thawing Siberian permafrost nearly fifty years ago and there have been others since then." She looked to Khan, worried. "What else do we know about it? And I don't mean the crap they print in the papers. What do we really know?"

Khan cleared his throat. "We know that it infected both archaeologists working on the body and quickly spread from there. For close to a week, authorities believed they had quarantined it in the mountain village. Until, that was, a case turned up in Hong Kong. An Asian student interning at the lab had gone home to visit his family before anyone knew how serious the situation was. The Chinese have been struggling to keep it under wraps, but the virus is spreading fast and picking up speed. It wasn't long after the original quarantine failed that a second wave began spreading through parts of northern Spain and southern France."

Now Riese wasn't the only one who seemed concerned.

"The mortality rate is close to ninety percent," Khan went on, "with symptoms that include headache, nausea and hemorrhaging from every orifice."

Images of the infected appeared on the screens behind them.

The room grew deathly quiet. Anders cringed from the horrific sight. "But why's it called Pyrenean hemorrhagic fever?" he asked.

Khan folded his hands. "It was named after the Spanish part of the Pyrenees mountain range in which it was discovered."

Riese shook her head. "Spain isn't liking the name one bit, I can assure you. Last century when HIV was first discovered, it was named GRID for 'gay-related

36

immune deficiency,' a mistake that inevitably led to homophobic slurs."

"I'm afraid," Khan said, "that the Spanish do not have a say in the matter. What does matter is the danger it poses. If the symptoms and the death rate weren't bad enough, those who manage to beat the odds and survive the infection are left with irreversible sterility."

Hovering by Khan's left shoulder, Meadows spoke up for the first time. "We've run the projections many times. The sterility is a game-changer. Judging from its current rate of infection, if the virus isn't stopped within ninety-six hours, it'll mean the end of mankind."

"Look, Mr. Khan," Anders said. "I appreciate the fifty up front for hearing you out, but I think you may have got your wires crossed. You're looking at a bunch of archaeologists and anthropologists. Hell, Erwin over there's a paleobotanist, which makes him twice as useless as the rest of us. And then there's Riese. She may have anger issues, but she's probably the only person qualified to lend a hand."

"Forty-eight hours ago," Khan said, ignoring him, "we received word from Gihon that they'd isolated a workable vaccine."

Riese's face scrunched up. "Gihon?"

"Our bioresearch facility," Khan told her.

Anders smirked. "So named after the second river said to flow from the Garden of Eden."

Khan nodded. "Correct."

Khazanov tried to lighten the mood. "I knew I should have paid attention in Sunday school."

"Then I don't see the problem," Anders told them. "Once you get the vaccine into production you'll be able to reset your little doomsday clock."

"I only wish it were that simple," Meadows explained. "This morning at 0900 hours Gihon went offline and we aren't sure why. What we need—what we're asking for you to do—is accompany our search-and-rescue team to the compound in order to reestablish contact."

Khazanov let out a lungful of air. "With all due respect, Mr. Khan, surely this is the first time any of us have heard of Gihon. How can we lead your men to a location when we don't even know where it is?"

A sly look formed on Khan's face. "Not so much where, Dr. Khazanov, but when."

Erwin rose from his seat, gripping the cherrywood table. "Oh, God, tell me you haven't…"

Khazanov's bellowing voice cut him off as he searched the room. "Am I the only one who's lost? What the heck does that mean—'not where, but when?'"

Khan's hands were clasped in front of him and Anders couldn't help noticing in that moment how much he looked like a funeral director.

Raising an arm, Khan motioned toward the sliding doors. "Allow me to show you."

Chapter 9

Khan led them through the bowels of the *Excelsior* to a room marked 'Stasis Chamber.' Round and dimly lit, it had a simple and utilitarian layout. Walls lined with banks of holographic monitors produced a dazzling array of lights. Technicians in white coveralls flitted like ghosts from one control panel to the next, punching in data and adjusting settings. The chamber was a symphony of ordered chaos and Anders' head began to ache. He caught sight of the raised platform in the center of the room.

Twelve pods arranged in a large circle.

Anders watched a female technician in a white protective suit pass by. "Anyone else feel a little underdressed?"

Khan raised his hand toward the high-tech equipment around them. "Steel may have made me rich," he told them. "But this is where we changed the world."

They all looked around at the impressive array of equipment.

"We think of time as an unalterable force forever marching forward. In this line of thinking, the past is set and the future pristine and unmapped. But what if I were to tell you that your senses have been lying to you?"

"First, I would wonder what you'd been smoking," Khazanov answered flatly.

Glancing at the pods, Riese said, "I thought this was going to be about space."

"This has nothing to do with space," Khan told her, "and everything to do with time."

Erwin's ears perked up. "I was afraid you were going to say that."

"We aren't only saying it," Meadows replied sharply. "We're doing it."

"But time travel isn't possible," Riese protested. "And I'm not talking about the kind that involves getting into a spaceship and flying around a black hole so you come back a few hundred years in the future. That's never been questioned. But going into the past…"

Khan laughed. "We came to discover, quite by accident, that brilliant men like Newton and Einstein were wrong. Time doesn't flow like a river, nor is it the fourth dimension. Time, at least as we've come to understand it, does not exist."

Anders wasn't sure if he heard Khan correctly. "Come again?"

"From a subatomic perspective," Khan explained, "the past, present and future are nothing more than events our brains have ordered according to an agreed-upon reality. Contrary to how our rational minds process the world around us, each of those moments is occurring at once. Our lives are made up of a series of nows happening simultaneously."

Erwin slapped his forehead, making a loud smack. "Am I dreaming or did everyone just go insane?"

40

"To be quite honest," Khan continued, "it wasn't our intention to trash the theory of time. We were trying to prove that teleportation beyond the subatomic level was not only possible but made good economic sense. This new understanding of a time-free universe was really nothing more than an accidental by-product. Learning to travel from one now to the next, that was the hard part."

"One now to the next," Khazanov repeated, bewildered.

Binh's head sank into his hands.

Anders was starting to wonder whether all of this had simply been an elaborate hoax.

"Think of it this way, Dr. Khazanov," Khan said as he strode over to a table, scooped up a thick technical manual and cracked the spine. "Imagine you're in the middle of your favorite hardcopy novel. From your point of view, the page you're on is the present. The pages before are your past, and everything yet unread your future. And yet the book exists as a finished whole, a series of nows waiting to be experienced. It is only because our brains process information at a given, predictable rate that you see time as having anything to do with it. But of course the analogy isn't perfect, because as we know the future isn't fixed. But neither is the past. Anything along the continuum can have an impact, although most of us would never know it since the narrative always appears consistent."

Difficult to grasp as it was, Anders felt like he was beginning to understand what Khan was saying. "So what we call the paranormal, things like ghosts…"

Khan set the book down. "Nothing more than bleedthroughs from a parallel moment in time."

Riese raised her hand and then quickly lowered it. "Next you're gonna start babbling about aliens."

"Those are a different matter altogether," Khan told her, his face lighting up.

"That's right, they're complete bullshit," Erwin blurted out and then cackled with laughter at his own humorless joke.

Meadows shook her head. "We believe they're visitors, perhaps studying what they think of as the past."

"You mean they're us?" Khazanov said.

Khan nodded. "We think so."

"Cool," Binh said, in broken English.

The mood in the room had become electric. Khan was describing a world that challenged everything they knew to be true.

"This bioresearch facility you mentioned," Riese said. "What can you tell us about it?"

"We call it the third doorway," he replied.

Erwin's eyebrows went up with surprise. "There's more than one?"

"To date we've been able to locate three unique P.I.N.T.S.," Khan explained, activating a monitor on the wall behind them. An image came up of what looked like a long funnel with two openings. "That's short for points in none-time and space."

"That makes sense," Anders said with a healthy dose of sarcasm.

Khan grew more serious. "We sent robotic monitors and later men into the first two doorways, but nothing ever returned. The third doorway was different, much different and it was there that we established our bioresearch laboratory. Gihon. The facility I'm asking you to get back for me." He motioned to the pods. "And these are the devices that will help send you there."

"Those pods of yours look more like coffins," Anders said, incredulous.

"When and where is this laboratory?" Riese asked, ignoring him.

Meadows cleared her throat before answering. "Not too far off the coast of Portugal. But nailing down an exact date has been far more difficult. Based on the ocean levels and retreating glaciers on the European continent, our closest estimates are 10,500 BCE."

The pen Anders had been fiddling with tumbled to the floor with a clang. His eyes widened as he drew the link between the historical location of the lab and the underwater site he'd been excavating off the coast of Portugal. Suddenly the modern objects he had found resting on the ocean floor for thousands of years began to make sense. With his heart pounding in his chest, Anders' gaze shifted to the stasis modules on the raised platform. He'd agreed to hear Khan out, but the more he listened, the more this was all becoming too much. "Am I the only one who thinks this is crazy? You're asking us to crawl into those torpedo tubes so you can fire us twelve thousand years into the past."

Erwin tisked. "Time doesn't exist, weren't you listening?"

"I'm afraid the initial entry point is closed," Khan informed them. "Because of that we have little choice but to insert you into an alternate location. We'll aim for the closest possible landmass, of course."

Anders was shaking his head. "Of course you will. That's all terribly reassuring, Mr. Khan, but—"

"Please keep in mind you'll be accompanied by a highly trained team. As experts in your respective fields, your roles will be purely advisory. Except for Riese, who will be tasked with identifying and collecting the vaccine. You'll be inserted along with all the gear and transportation you'll need." On the display screen, an image of a Cutter appeared. "Once you reestablish contact with Gihon, my men will repair the anomaly which caused the problem in the first place. Believe me, you'll be back before you know it." He paused and

43

glanced down at his feet, then back up at them. "I'm offering each of you a once-in-a-lifetime opportunity to see with your very own eyes a world you've only glimpsed through textbooks and computer simulations. I'm offering you a meeting with destiny. I know that once you return, you'll be begging to go back."

Anders surveyed the three scientists sitting next to him, each of them practically vibrating with anticipation. Maybe Khan was right. Maybe the mission would be a cakewalk, a once-in-a-lifetime chance to see the past like never before. But Khan wasn't the one going back, risking his life. Anders rose to his feet. He'd made up his mind.

"Thank you for the offer, Khan, but Binh and I are out. We'll take our chances with the virus."

The shift in Binh's expression made it clear Anders didn't speak for both of them.

Khan also looked surprised. "Are you sure about this, Dr. Anders? Perhaps you'd like some time to think things through?"

"Well, since I've come to understand that all time is simultaneous, I've already given it some thought and my answer is still no."

Shaking his head with disappointment, Khan said, "I'm truly sorry to hear that. A plane will take you back in the morning. Ms. Meadows will lead you to your quarters."

Anders, Meadows and a reluctant Binh headed toward the exit.

"I guess what they said about you is true," Riese called out after him.

Anders stopped, his hand hovering over the open door switch. Part of him knew what she was about to say, but he asked anyway. "Oh, and what is that?"

"That when the chips are down you're the first to cut and run. You heard what they said. In ninety-six hours the virus will reach the point of no return. After that it won't matter what relics you scoop off the ocean floor."

He punched the door switch and was on his way out, Binh right behind him, when Erwin leaned into Riese.

"Don't worry," he told her. "I'll take care of you."

He was about to put his arm around her when Riese said, "Just try it, plant-man. I dare you."

Flinching, Erwin retracted his arm and set it at his side.

Chapter 10

An hour later Anders was trying to fall asleep when he caught loud music coming from Binh's cabin next door. He marched into the hallway, feeling the first signs of a headache beginning to take hold, and banged on his neighbor's door. A second later, Binh appeared along with thick clouds of cigarette smoke which billowed into the corridor. From inside the room came the mellow groove of Bob Marley's *Buffalo Soldier.*

"The hell is going on in there?" Anders shouted, waving at tendrils of smoke. He pushed past Binh and into the room without waiting for an answer. A duffel bag sat atop his bunk, overflowing with bottles of booze.

"You wanna explain where you got all this stuff?"

Binh told him.

"Are you crazy? What's gonna happen when Khan goes into his office and finds his things are missing? I distinctly remember telling you not to steal anything." Then something in Binh's bag caught Anders' attention. "Is that a bottle of Hennessy?"

Binh nodded, lighting a new cigarette from the old one.

Anders grabbed the bottle of cognac and regarded it with admiration before he reached in and snatched another.

After a quiet whimper, Binh shared his thoughts on the expedition Khan had proposed.

"Of course it's insane," Anders shot back. "The others are so busy thinking about the scholarly articles they'll publish to consider that this may be a one-way trip. Besides, survival of the fittest, right?"

Binh looked doubtful.

That last part had come out quickly and even Anders wasn't sure he believed it himself.

"You're worried about the virus," Anders said and it was more statement than question.

Binh nodded, ashing his cigarette on the carpet.

Anders watched the gray clump crumple as it hit the ground, his face contorted in a frown. Anders was starting to feel the crushing weight of guilt for abandoning the group. He'd walked away from Dr. Hiddenger too, after he'd lost faith in the direction they were headed. Their friendship destroyed over a professional difference of opinion. It was a decision that hung over him whenever he closed his eyes at night. His mentor had been left alone to weather the storm of ridicule and name-calling far too frequent in the academic community. Sometimes standing alone was tough. But sometimes staying the course was tougher.

Anders went to the door, both bottles of Hennessy in hand. "You just make sure you're up tomorrow at the crack of dawn or I'm leaving without you."

•••

Back in his cabin, Anders fetched a cup from the bathroom and poured himself a stiff drink. The room was just spacious enough for a bunk at one end and a small table and chair at the other. And that was where he sat, tilting his glass and wiping his lips with the back of his hand after each drink. Before him was the gift from his mother. He set the glass down and tore off the wrapping paper. Inside he found a small, nondescript box. He held it to his ear and shook. Unlike a wallet, this had some weight to it.

Unable to divine the contents, he peeled back the lid and reached in. His fingers closed around a metallic object which he removed and held up to the light. Startled, he realized it was a wrist watch, made of silver with gold hands, sporting a tiny compass on the face. The craftsmanship was impressive, but Anders wasn't much for bling. Besides, watches as time-telling devices had become obsolete decades ago. He tossed it on the table where it landed with a loud thud.

Out came the Hennessy again, along with a clink as the neck touched the glass and a flood of delicious cognac flowed to the brim. Anders brought it to his lips and was about to wash it down when something caught his eye. He lowered the glass into a small puddle of spilled booze, his hand betraying a slight tremble.

There was an inscription on the underside of the watch's case cover. Heart beating like a drum, Anders rushed to his bag and rooted past shirts, underwear and socks until he found the shorts he'd been wearing earlier. Inside the pocket was the printout he'd made on the *Lady Luck* with the X-ray wand, the one showing the object Sykes had sent up from the depths of the Atlantic.

Anders peeled it open and studied the grainy image.

The letters on the printout— *IND WH*—hadn't made a lick of sense when he first saw them. But now, comparing the image from the X-ray to the watch lying on the table, he was witnessing something unimaginable. The two seemed to match.

May you find what you seek.

Surely he must be imagining things. He searched the X-ray for more clues and quickly found one, a tiny string of numbers etched along the bottom of the case cover. In the image they were far too worn to make out, except for the final digit, a seven, his lucky number. He plucked the watch off the table and studied the same area. The long list of numbers was there and so too was the seven, right at the end.

A pair of bony fingers danced up his spine and his first blinding impulse was to open the porthole window and toss the damned thing into the ocean. There was something so incredibly surreal about all of this that Anders was having a hard time wrapping his head around it. If nothing else, the implications left little room for doubt. Hadn't Khan said that the biolab was close to where Anders and his team had been scouring the ocean floor for artifacts? The same spot where they'd dredged up those two strange objects.

It meant that somehow this watch, his watch, had made the twelve-thousand-five-hundred-year journey into the past, where it had ended up at the bottom of the ocean.

A million questions raced through his beleaguered mind. He fell back onto his bunk, the watch still gripped tightly in his hand. He was at a crossroads, perhaps the biggest of his life. He could do as he'd said he would and return with Binh in the morning. Return to a world on the brink of death. Or he could ride one of those stasis tubes straight into the rabbit hole and see firsthand what lay on the other side.

Anders drew in a deep breath, realizing the decision had already been made. And with that, he undid the metallic strap and slid the watch onto his wrist.

Chapter 11

The mission briefing was held in the hold of the ship, a cavernous, cathedral-like space lined with large containers and crates of supplies. Anders and Binh arrived to find that the others were already there. A handful of chairs sat facing a digital whiteboard. Placed between the two were tables cluttered with gear. In the background was a Cutter. In spite of the craft's size, it was swallowed by the enormity of the space.

Meadows stopped the briefing as they approached. Seated with the other scientists, Riese was fighting hard to hide her astonishment. Next to her, Khazanov smiled broadly. Not surprisingly, Erwin's face soured at Anders' arrival.

Standing off to the side were four mean-looking mercenary types in black tactical gear.

"Glad you could make it," Khazanov said. "The bus nearly left without you."

"We weren't sure whether we'd see you again," Meadows said with a happy jingle in her voice, or at least what might have passed for one in a woman who didn't show much emotion.

"Neither was I," Anders admitted, distinctly aware of the watch secured around his wrist. "I guess you could say I had a sudden change of heart."

A hint of a smile appeared on Riese's face as he and Binh settled into a seat and waited for Meadows to continue. Despite her calm demeanor, Anders recognized fear on her brave face. The allure of seeing the past first hand was hard to deny, but so too was the danger of never coming back.

"These are the men who will be accompanying you," Meadows told them. She pointed to the first merc: a gruff, olive-skinned soldier sporting a brush cut and a goatee. *If looks could kill,* Anders thought, *the four of us would long be dead.*

"Vacek is your team leader," Meadows told them. "He's been a loyal Genesis employee for many years. If anyone has the skills to keep you safe and bring you home in one piece, it's him."

Vacek nodded, flexing the muscles in his powerful jaw.

The next merc in line stepped forward. He was short, wiry and seemed to be swearing under his breath. "Halloway was a medic in the army for nearly ten years before joining us." Meadows paused, holding out a hand to reassure them. "Not that anyone will get hurt."

The sound of polite, but nervous laughter was drowned out by the giant space they were in.

A handsome white soldier with a shaved head and sparkling childlike eyes gave the scientists a half-wave.

"This is Stills. He's a communications specialist and engineer. If it's broken, Stills can fix it."

Halloway punched Stills in the shoulder. "Hear that? She's making you sound like a damn hero."

The soldiers laughed.

"And this," Meadows said, pointing to a muscular black merc who was wearing a deep grimace, "is Castleman. Weapons specialist, scout and all-round nice guy."

A low growl of disapproval emanated from Castleman.

"Yeah," Anders said. "He looks like a real charmer."

Halloway turned to Castleman. "More dead weight," the medic said without making much effort to keep the others from hearing.

Castleman clenched his teeth as his gaze settled on Anders.

"Five minutes in and Anders is already making friends," Riese observed. "Maybe if we're lucky they'll leave you back in ten thousand BCE."

"Only if I'm lucky," Anders replied, wondering if he was the only one who had considered the very real dangers of the mission they were embarking on.

Behind Meadows, a holographic map rose up from a display cube on the table, highlighting the coast of Portugal. She pointed to an open field a few miles inland.

"This is where you'll be inserted, along with a fully equipped Cutter," she informed them. "Everything you'll need for the journey will be stowed away inside the ship. We'll also outfit each of you with packs containing a few essentials."

Erwin raised his hand.

"You have a question?" Meadows asked.

He repositioned his glasses. "Yeah, maybe it's nothing, but if this is such a straight-arrow mission, why do you need us?"

She smiled politely. "To tell you the truth, apart from Riese, you people are part of the contingency plan. The men accompanying you are specialists in search-and-rescue operations. You folks are experts in the sights and sounds of the Neolithic period. If you should encounter anything anomalous, we wanted to ensure at least one of you would have a frame of reference. But if you're worried at all about research, let me assure you, once you arrive on the island, you'll have plenty of time to study the vast array of indigenous species."

"What the pretty lady's trying to say," Halloway piped up, "is better to have you and not want you than to want you and not have you. Capiche?"

"Get these people geared up and ready to go," Meadows ordered Vacek coldly. "You drop in thirty minutes."

Chapter 12

Vacek stood before a table littered with equipment, much of it tagged with orange stickers labeled 'Property of Genesis Corporation.' The scientists and Binh were each dressed in navy blue coveralls and matching boots.

"Your outfits are a composite fabric made with carbon nanoparticles," Vacek told them. "Whatever natural environment you enter, this material will morph to help you blend in, much like the skin of an octopus."

Anders glanced down at his sleeve, waiting for something to happen.

"Heads up, hotshot," Vacek said as he tossed Anders a vest. Anders caught it with one hand. Vacek was impressed. "Good reflexes." He turned back to the others. "Go ahead and put these on. They're all-purpose safety vests, rated to stop most pistol and even some rifle rounds. Should you decide to take a swim, simply pull both of these cords. The vest will inflate and you'll bob to the surface like a cork."

"Riese won't need one," Khazanov said, as Vacek reached out to hand her a vest. "She was on the Olympic swim team."

Vacek raised an eyebrow.

"I wasn't on the team," Riese corrected him. "I was offered a spot and turned it down."

"Well, excuse us," Anders replied.

Vacek handed her the vest anyway. "The backpacks we've prepared for each of you have already been outfitted with most of the essentials, MREs—"

Erwin leaned into Khazanov. "MRE?"

"Meals ready to eat," Anders told him. "Basically a pouch with nasty food. Been around for over a hundred years. Stick the sealed part into the heating pouch, pour in some water and a chemical reaction will heat the food in a few minutes."

Erwin opened the packsack resting at his feet, dropped in his camera and fished out an MRE. He held the label up so he could read it. "Veggie burger," he said with acute disappointment. "Anyone wanna trade? Anyone?"

Vacek held a large blue pill between his index finger and thumb. "Each of you will take one of these. We call them big boys and they're filled with nanites which will enable us to track you within a fifty-mile radius." Vacek indicated the OLED (organic light-emitting diode) display on his wrist.

"That pill's the size of a gobstopper," Riese protested. "I'll never get it down. You must have something else."

Vacek winked at her. "Sorry, sweetheart, but there ain't no GPS in the Garden of Eden."

Riese cocked an eyebrow, looking thoroughly unimpressed before she took the pill from him. One by

56

one, they placed them in their mouths and swallowed. Riese's eyes watered as she fought to get it down.

On the table were what looked like sleek black pistols.

"Tell me we get one of those." Erwin reached his hand out.

Vacek smacked it away with a tisk. "I don't like children who grab," he said, then to the rest of the group. "Our mandate prevents us from doing any unnecessary harm. That goes for the wildlife as well as the natives. And trust me, the last thing you wanna do is kill off your great-grandfather ten thousand times removed. That's why these weapons are an absolute last resort. They're not so much stun guns as they are neural inhibitors." Vacek lifted one off the table and pointed it at empty space. "A single blast from this pop gun'll drop a wooly mammoth in under three seconds. While it may not kill him, he'll sure wake up with one hell of a hangover. A shot at point-blank range can be lethal so be careful."

Binh looked positively elated.

Anders wasn't sure about all this. "A little overkill, don't you think?"

Vacek's facial features fell. "Not where we're going."

•••

After the briefing and equipment check, Vacek and his team led the scientists back to the stasis chamber. From there, technicians dressed in white cleanroom suits enclosed each of the team members inside their respective vertical translucent tube. The open space around which the pods were arranged was now occupied by a Cutter vehicle, also encased in a special shell.

Anders glanced down at his watch, distinctly aware they had ninety-four hours to complete their mission.

Across from him, he spotted Erwin, looking like a man about to shit his pants. Binh was locked into the pod next door, wearing a smile reserved for a man about to crest the peak of a rollercoaster ride.

Vacek, Stills, Castleman and Halloway didn't appear the least bit scared. Then Anders spotted Riese and the beads of sweat rolling down her forehead. He caught her eye and winked, to which she replied with a weak smile.

Once all nine members of the team were locked in, a display on the wall above them began the countdown.

Twenty seconds… nineteen… eighteen…

•••

In the control room overlooking the stasis chamber, technicians seated at multicolored consoles monitored fluctuations in the chamber's gravitational field. Khan and Meadows stood peering out from the observation porthole. Khan's fingers, laced behind his back, fidgeted as they always did when he was nervous.

Meadows became aware of it and asked, "What do you think their chances are?"

On the board, the seconds ticked away.

Six… five… four…

The room began to tremble as the powerful gravity amplifiers on the ceiling were brought to bear. Their activation was accompanied by an audible hum just shy of causing discomfort. Imperceptibly at first, the chamber began to fill with blue smoke. Thin strands of electrical discharge licked up between the tubes. The amplifiers were growing in strength, tearing open the Einstein-Rosen Bridge that linked the two coordinates together.

58

"Given that every other team we've sent back has failed," Khan replied, his face awash with blue light, "I'd say their chances are slim to none."

Three... two... one...

The reactive glass separating the control booth from the stasis chamber tinted protectively as the chamber exploded with a massive coronal discharge. If Khan had blinked, he would have missed the figures in the tubes, along with the aircraft positioned between them, seemingly stretched as they were sucked through the floor.

"Godspeed," he whispered, unable to shake the feeling that he'd seen them for the last time.

Chapter 13

94 hours remaining

A burst of pain fired through every nerve ending in his body. That was the first sensation Anders became aware of. The second was being high in the air, twenty, maybe thirty feet up, looking down on a body of azure-blue water. His arms and legs were bicycling wildly, the wind screaming in his ears. This wasn't a dream. This was real life and he was falling through midair.

A moment before impact, his legs clamped together. Water rushed over him as he plunged deeper, everything slow and labored now, sounds muffled and distorted.

He wasn't a great swimmer and Anders' lungs cried out for oxygen, his diaphragm contracting painfully. His body wanted to breathe so badly it was even willing to pull in water if need be. An image of his life vest flashed before his eyes and he suddenly remembered what he had to do. Struggling, Anders pawed at his chest, searching for the elusive cords.

They were nowhere to be found. His vision began to darken. He was losing consciousness. Then a shape appeared and a pale, slender hand yanked hard, filling the water around him with bubbles. Seconds later, he broke the surface, gasping for air. He wasn't alone. Riese was beside him. She'd saved his life by inflating his vest.

Chaos reigned around them. Screams of terror rang out as more forms bobbed up. It wasn't supposed to be like this. They'd been told they would be set down in a field, not dropped into a lake or the sea or wherever the hell they were.

Twenty yards away, Erwin was treading water, clearly in shock, staring off into the distance.

"Erwin, get your ass over here," Anders barked, calling him again before he started to move. The paleobotanist fought the constraints of his life vest as he swam over. But he didn't get further than fifteen feet or so before a massive object crashed into the water behind him, sending chunks of metal and glass high into the air accompanied by a giant plume of water. Stunned, Erwin and the others nearby shielded their heads with their hands to protect from falling debris.

Anders watched the entire display with amazement until a stinging realization caught up with him.

That giant object he had seen disintegrate and sink beneath the surface had been their Cutter.

The aircraft that was supposed to fly them to the disabled island laboratory.

"Where's Vacek?" Riese asked, searching around.

Anders removed his vest and dropped beneath the surface, searching for signs of Vacek or anyone else who hadn't made it up.

Riese did the same and that was when she spotted the limp figure sinking. She came up, took a deep breath and kicked, to get there in time. After closing the twenty feet that lay between them, Riese grabbed hold of Vacek's waist and pulled both cords on his vest. It inflated at once, propelling them to the surface.

They broke through, Vacek still unconscious.

"Hold on," she told him.

Shrugging back into his life vest, Anders had stayed behind to figure out where they were. Less than a hundred feet away he saw a shoreline. It seemed they'd been dumped into a lake.

Anders swam over and helped her bring Vacek ashore. He was conscious by the time they arrived. With their help he rolled over on all fours, vomiting water from his lungs.

Halloway swooped in to administer aid.

Anders found Riese, brushing sand off her knees. "I see now why Khazanov was so sure you'd been on the Olympic team."

She started to smile and then stopped herself. "Don't mention it. I like to think you'd have done the same for me."

The group remained on the beach, gathering whatever gear they could. A quick check revealed that everyone was banged up and badly shaken, but accounted for.

"Anyone wanna tell me what the hell happened back there?" Erwin shouted. He was still wearing his life vest, which had since deflated.

"A miscalculation," Vacek sputtered, now on his feet. He seemed preoccupied, beyond the fact that he'd nearly drowned.

"A miscalculation?" Erwin spat, incredulous.

He spun toward the diminutive scientist. "What else can I tell you? Obviously this wasn't part of the plan."

Halloway unholstered his neural inhibitor and shook the water out. Stills did the same and then held his up for a test fire.

"Don't bother," Halloway advised. "Thing's waterlogged."

Stills swore and put it back.

A few feet on, Erwin still wasn't done bitching. "Am I the only one who's noticed that all our equipment's at the bottom of the damn lake?"

"Erwin, take it easy," Anders said, trying to ease the situation. "We're all in the same boat here."

"Yeah, lucky for us." Vacek said, pivoting to scan the lake again. A few seconds went by before he said, "What are those?"

Thirty yards out, a group of packs were jostling in the current.

Khazanov ran into the water and swam out to retrieve them. Vacek motioned to Halloway, Stills and Castleman to go help.

They returned a few minutes later. Breathing heavily, they tossed the packs onto the wet sand. The fabric was waterproof and watertight, which had meant once the ship had come apart, they'd bobbed to the surface. Some of the other debris was beginning to wash ashore.

Erwin grabbed his pack and started wiping the sand off it. "So what now, oh great leader? Build a campfire and sing kumbaya?"

Vacek stepped toward Erwin with the look of a man about to squash a bug. "First things first, little man, you're gonna shut your mouth."

Anders stood between them. "Go easy, Vacek, he's still in shock."

"This isn't the time to be crying over spilled milk," Khazanov stated in his thick Russian accent. "What we need to do is figure out where we are and—"

The swish of a spear cutting through the air was followed by a thud as it buried itself in Khazanov's leg.

He cried out in pain, grasping at the wound. On instinct, the mercs each drew their sidearms, except for Halloway, who dropped next to Khazanov and began pulling the spear from his leg and applying a tourniquet. In a flash, Erwin and Riese fell in behind the others. Anders stood with the soldiers, his hand hovering over the neural inhibitor holstered on his hip.

Encircling the beach on all sides was a dense row of tropical vegetation. His pulse pounding, Anders scanned the dark edges, looking for a sign of where that spear might have come from.

"Anyone see anything?" Stills shouted, his shaved head glistening with sweat. The sun was high, baking each of them to a fine crisp. They'd have to get off this beach sooner or later.

Castleman's eyes were fearful, flickering back and forth. "I don't see shit, man. Just a bunch of trees."

As he spoke, ghostly figures emerged from the edge of the forest—a group of short, but robust-looking men carrying spears, their skin covered with white ash and animal skins. Others among them were painted with vibrant colors. Many of them wore objects around their heads made from leaves and dried weeds plucked from the lake. One figure on the end had branches draped over his head, bearing exotic fruit. They kept their distance, speaking amongst each other in a guttural language. Soon, a heated discussion ensued.

"What the hell is going on?" Erwin squealed, holding onto Riese for dear life. She shoved him away.

"I say we waste 'em," Castleman told Vacek.

The mercenary leader shook his head. "With what? Before that weapon of yours even has a chance to misfire, we'll all be dead."

"The hell are those savages saying, man?" Stills asked, fighting the panic so evident in his voice.

Khazanov winced with pain. "They're trying to figure out who we are and whether we're—" He stopped himself. "Edible."

"Edible?" Castleman repeated in disbelief.

"Tell them I taste like shit, will you," Erwin said.

Riese didn't waste a beat. "I'm sure they can tell."

"How do you know what they're saying?" Vacek demanded.

The Russian laughed. "Buy me a drink later and I'll be happy to explain."

More robust men with eerily painted faces emerged from the forest's edge.

Standing now with their backs to the water, the group found themselves surrounded on all sides.

"You still think we should stand down, boss?" Castleman asked, checking his weapon and finding that it hadn't yet come back online.

A native with an ornate headdress came forward, waving his spear. He addressed them in a garbled tongue that sounded like nonsense.

Halloway helped Khazanov, now bandaged, to his feet.

"I believe they want us to go with them," the Russian said, favoring his left leg where the spear had entered.

"So what do we do?" Stills asked, looking at the others.

Anders swallowed hard. "We do as they say."

Chapter 14

The haze and meaty odor from cooking fires drifted over the village as the prisoners were led into camp. At once, Anders took note of the unusual huts set in a circular pattern around a central fire pit. He had seen similar structures made of mammoth bones near Mezhyrich, Ukraine, dating back some fifteen thousand years, but nothing of the sort had ever been discovered this far west.

Kneeling by the main fire pit, three women draped in animal skins were busy stripping the flesh from what appeared to be a human skull, or at least humanoid. But it wasn't simply the grisly sight of the de-fleshing which caught Anders' attention, nor the unusual curves on the skull, it was the mishmash of tools the women were using. Two of them were wielding flint scrapers while the third sliced away the pinkish goo with a beat-up Bowie knife.

To the left of the main hut stood what looked to Anders like a totem pole. The trunk of a tree had been

66

recessed into the ground and carved to form a series of images. Far from crude, the images highlighted a level of artistry which surprised even him. A handful of those near the top, normally a spot reserved for gods and lesser deities, showed what appeared to be ships and men emerging from inside them.

As they were marched further into the village, they spotted children covered only in white ash and patches of mud. They had been chasing each other about, shouting and playing games, but now they stood rooted in place, staring in awe. More figures emerged from huts, some elderly, others young and muscular.

It was still unclear where they'd landed and who these people were. Apart from the elaborate decorations, Anders could see they were Caucasian, some with short powerful builds and prominent brow ridges. They looked a hell of a lot like Neanderthals, although he knew that wasn't possible. By thirty thousand BCE, Neanderthals were already extinct.

From out of nowhere, a group of adolescent males wearing animal-skin loincloths and medium-sized headdresses stalked up to Riese and grabbed hold of her arms. She shrieked with fear and resisted fiercely as they began trying to separate her from the group. Khazanov and Anders immediately moved in to stop them, wedging themselves between Riese and the men as she swore and kicked at them. More warriors moved in, waving sharpened flint-tipped spears.

One of the warriors shouted with a crazed expression as he shoved the edge of a flint knife against Anders' throat. It stung as it grazed his flesh and drew blood. Flint blades might be primitive, but that didn't make them any less sharp. Despite the dangers facing them, Anders and Khazanov continued trying to fend off the young men's attempts to take Riese.

"Let them have her or we'll all be dead," Vacek snapped.

Hearing that only made Riese scream louder.

Anders threw Vacek an incredulous look as he struggled to hold on. "I'll remember that when they're about to turn your head into an ashtray." Then to Khazanov: "For God's sake, tell them to back off."

Khazanov spoke up in a garbled dialect that bore only a passing resemblance to the native language Anders had heard them speaking before.

Hearing Khazanov's words, the natives stopped dead, stunned into silence. Then seemingly at once, they erupted into fits of laughter. Even the older women by the camp fire, droopy-breasted and toothless, joined in. The woman with the Bowie knife pointed it at Khazanov as she howled.

The Russian shrugged. "Not exactly the reaction I was going for."

•••

They released Riese after that, choosing instead to imprison the nine team members in a large bamboo cage, the door secured with vines. Their bags had been confiscated too and were presently being rummaged through by the natives. Khazanov stood near the entrance, listening to them fight over the spoils they'd collected. One of them came out wearing his long underwear as though it were a shirt.

Across from Khazanov Anders sat with his back pressed against the wooden slats, his eyes closed. He was trying to catch some quick shuteye when a fly tickled his cheek. He swatted it away only to feel it once again. This time he opened his eyes and bolted upright when he saw it wasn't a fly at all. The young native boy he'd seen on the beach was squatting outside the bars beside him, grinning as he poked him in the cheek with a twig. Unlike many of the other children he'd seen in the village, this boy had soft and angular features, with blue eyes and dirty blond hair, and a frame which appeared stouter than an average modern male child his age. In a quiet voice he spoke to Anders, who didn't understand a word he was saying.

"Sorry, kid, I don't speak Neanderthal." Anders pointed at Khazanov. "There's the guy you wanna talk to."

They glanced over to see more of their clothing being worn by the natives, much of it in the wrong way. Socks as mittens, underwear as hats.

"He isn't Neanderthal," Khazanov said, wincing from the pain in his leg. "Not completely, at least."

Anders rubbed his cheek. "Coulda fooled me."

The Russian looked at Riese. "Is the handheld DNA sequencer still in your pack?"

Riese shook her head and reached into a cargo pocket. She came out with the device and switched it on, not seeming to expect much given the swim they'd just taken. "Well, it's working."

Halloway snorted. "It'd be nice if our inhibitors were as reliable."

Vacek threw him a look.

"I'm saying for next time."

"We don't figure out how to get free and there won't be a next time," Anders said, distinctly aware the child was still hunched in his peripheral vision, hanging on his every word.

"Think you can get a sample of his blood?" Khazanov asked Riese.

"No, but I think Anders could."

Anders rolled his eyes and snatched the sequencer out of Riese's grasp.

"Hit the red button, then press the end to the pad of his index finger," she told him.

"Khazanov," Anders said. "Tell the kid to hold out his hand."

The Russian swallowed down the obvious pain in his leg and said a few words to the boy. His head tilted as Khazanov spoke. He giggled, but did nothing.

Binh suggested maybe the kid needed a bribe.

Maybe Binh had a point. Anders took hold of the Genesis patch on his shoulder and tore it off. He then extended his hand to the boy and offered it to him. Given that the necklace the boy wore contained a clump of hair tied with a piece of metal wire and an adult molar, Anders figured the patch might just be eclectic enough to work.

The native boy took Anders' gift and tucked it away. When he was done, he held out his hand. Anders lowered the tip of the DNA sequencer over his index finger and pressed the red button. The boy yelped and yanked his hand away.

Anders tossed the device over to Riese while the boy sucked the blood from his puncture wound.

"Ask the kid if he has a name," Anders said.

Khazanov did so and grinned at the boy's response. "He says his name is Aku. It means 'cleansing water.'"

The sequencer in Riese's hand buzzed and beeped as it worked through the boy's genome.

"The necklace," Anders said. "Find out where he got it."

After a brief discussion, Khazanov told him. "He says these were items which used to belong to his mother. He says she's gone, returned to the great lake."

Anders reached through and felt the tuft of hair on Aku's necklace.

Riese watched him do this with surprise. "I have the results," she said at last.

70

"I can't wait," Khazanov said, rubbing his hands together.

"According to this, he's fifty-one percent *Homo sapiens* and forty-nine percent Neanderthal," she told them.

"A hybrid," Erwin blurted out.

Anders didn't look impressed. "That's one way of putting it." He locked eyes with Khazanov. "His mother must have been *Homo sapiens*, perhaps kidnapped by the tribe."

The Russian agreed. "Which means most of the others are likely full Neanderthal—they do have the flared lower ribcage, the squat build and the heavy brow ridgeline."

"Except if this really is ten thousand five hundred BCE," Riese piped up, "Neanderthals have already been extinct for nearly twenty thousand years."

"That's true," Erwin agreed, looking even more worried. "So how could that be?"

"It's not unheard of that Neanderthals may have continued to exist in small bands long after their currently agreed-upon expiration date," Khazanov explained. "Look at the *Homo floresiensis*. They were a parallel species to our own locked on an island habitat for thousands of years. We've also come to understand through genetic testing that at some point in our evolutionary past, humans and Neanderthals mated."

"He's got a point," Anders said, distinctly aware the blue-eyed boy was still staring at him. "I remember reading somewhere that Neanderthal DNA is what gave us white skin and straight hair, among other traits."

Vacek didn't look at all impressed. "The kid's half-human, half-Neanderthal? So he looks like a caveman and acts like the Viet Cong? Are you nearly done?"

"What I don't get," Stills said, "is how you know what they're saying."

71

Vacek threw Stills a harsh look, admonishing his engineer for encouraging them.

"I don't, not fully at least," Khazanov replied truthfully, still gripping the bars and favoring his bandaged leg. "Most of it is educated guesswork. Neolithic linguistics and vocalizations are my area, just like yours is guns and killing." The mercenaries shifted uncomfortably before the Russian carried on. "You see, all language evolves over time. In the same way that geneticists have been trying to clone dinosaurs by rolling back chicken DNA, we've spent the last thirty years doing the same with extinct languages. They're speaking an Afro-Asiatic language—an ancient cousin to the Berber tongue would be my closest guess. If so, then that puts us somewhere in North Africa and right around the right time frame."

Halloway snickered. "You sure about that?" the medic asked. "This doesn't look like a desert to me."

"That may be," Erwin cut in. "But keep in mind that the climate in the Sahara has shifted many times over the last twenty thousand years, from wet and fertile to dry and barren."

Castleman cracked his knuckles. "Lucky for us we were dropped out of the sky into a lake instead of a sand dune."

"All of this is real fascinating," Anders said, climbing to his feet. "But I'm not gonna wait here until they start getting hungry." He looked at Vacek. "How much longer until those pop guns of yours can fire?"

Vacek removed his weapon and studied it. "Hard to say. An hour, maybe more."

"That's too long," Anders replied. He moved the door and began shouting at one of the nearby warriors haggling over an MRE pillaged from one of their backpacks. "Hey, Bigfoot. Yeah, you, get over here."

Erwin pushed his back against the cage. "Anders, are you insane? You're going to get us killed."

From the corner of his mouth, Anders said, "Listen, I have an idea."

"Oh, how reassuring!" Riese said, taking Erwin's side. "Please tell me you're not going to fake a tummy ache and jump him when he comes to investigate."

The mercs snickered.

"Wasn't long ago they were trying to cart you off by your hair for a long romantic weekend," Anders reminded her before turning his attention back to the warrior. "Hey, Captain Caveman."

Riese balled up her hands until her knuckles turned white. "I should have let you drown when I had the chance."

Beside her, Binh nodded in agreement.

Anders caught the slight and pointed his thumb at Riese. "Don't encourage her, will ya? We already got enough problems as it is."

"Uh, Anders," Khazanov warned.

Anders turned back to find the ugly face of a village brute glaring back at him through the wooden slates. Clearly agitated, the warrior began shouting.

"All you're doing is pissing him off," Vacek said. "Keep your mouth shut and wait until sundown, then we'll get you out of here."

"Something tells me we won't last that long," Erwin said.

Eyes locked with the brute, Anders continued to taunt him. "Your breath smells like a sewer. Do you kiss your mother with that mouth?"

The warrior grunted and thrust the spear between the bars, just as Anders had hoped he would. In a quick motion, Anders sidestepped and grabbed hold of the spear. A violent tug of war ensued.

"Man, this guy's stronger than he looks," Anders said, holding on as best he could. Back and forth they went as Anders felt his face pulled into the wooden bars more than once. Outside, the warrior yanked on the spear, rocking to and fro when suddenly his body was lifted up and thrown several feet backwards, disappearing into a clump of bushes.

"Holy Superman," Erwin shouted in disbelief. "How the hell did you do that?"

Anders stood staring down at the spear shaft still in his hands, wondering the same thing.

All at once, screams of fear erupted from every part of the village. Natives dropped what they were holding and broke into a full run.

Suddenly Anders and the others became aware of the sound of thrusters overhead. A ship hovered above them, only partially visible through the thick forest canopy.

Open bay doors were visible underneath the craft, from which nets connected to lengths of rope were fired out in several directions at once. One became tangled up with the branches of a tree, but others hit their mark, scooping up large groups of villagers and pulling them into the ship's hold.

"Here comes the cavalry," Erwin shouted in triumph.

In a matter of seconds, the village was a ghost town. Those who hadn't been captured had fled into the safety of the dense jungle.

Slowly the ship began to move away.

"And there goes the cavalry," Anders observed, noticing for the first time that Aku was gone.

With a burst of panic, Erwin began flapping his arms, screaming at the ship. "Don't leave, we're down here."

Riese and Khazanov joined in.

74

A distinct look of alarm spread over Vacek's face.

In another few moments, the ship would be out of sight.

Frantic, Erwin kicked at the cage door, tearing at the vines holding it shut.

The big Russian pushed him aside. "Move."

"Wait," Vacek shouted.

Hobbling, Khazanov charged the door, looking as though adrenaline was surging through his veins. It gave at once, sending him tumbling to the ground. Erwin stormed out, trampling over Khazanov as he yelled for the pilot of the aircraft to stay.

For a moment, the ship lingered.

Still in the jail, Stills turned to Vacek. "What do we do, boss?"

The merc leader swore and ran out, tackling Erwin to the ground while the paleobotanist's arms were still waving through the air.

Erwin struggled to his feet and dusted himself off. "Are you crazy?" he screeched as the ship began circling around. "They may be our last chance for a rescue."

Anders, Khazanov and Riese moved in to support Erwin. For once, he was making sense. Not surprisingly, Stills, Castleman and Halloway squared with Vacek. A heated argument ensued.

Vacek held Erwin's arm with one hand and pointed to the hut with the other. "All of you shut up and get out of sight."

"Have you lost your mind?" Anders asked, incredulous.

"Get off me, will you?" Erwin whined, squirming out of Vacek's iron grasp.

"Do it," Vacek replied. "And fast."

The low hum of thrusters roared as the ship came about, positioned over the village again. Glancing up at it between the cage slates, Anders noticed that it bore a striking resemblance to the Cutter they'd been sent back with. The same one now sitting at the bottom of the lake.

"You wanna tell us what the hell's going on, Vacek?" Anders demanded.

"Simple rescue mission, my ass," Erwin spat. "A once-in-a-lifetime opportunity," he said, imitating Khan's Indian accent. "This wasn't what I signed up for."

Stills, Castleman and Halloway peered up through the gaps in the walls as the ship circled over the village. They looked like men hiding from the law.

"Never thought I'd say this," Riese admitted. "But I agree with Erwin."

Vacek stayed low, urging the others to do the same. "Believe me, getting dropped into the drink was definitely not part of the plan. But we gotta play the cards we're dealt, not the ones we wish we had."

"Let's stick to the point for a moment, shall we," Anders said. "That ship might have been our only hope of getting home."

"I doubt that very much," Vacek countered.

Erwin sighed. "Oh, do you?" He swiveled toward the others in disbelief, his voice growing more emphatic. "Then you probably doubt we're up to our eyeballs in shit." He tapped his hand against his forehead in what might have been a salute.

"What makes you so certain, Vacek?" Riese asked, willing to hear him out.

"I can tell by the markings on that ship," the merc leader replied. "It isn't one of ours."

Chapter 15

Ali Khan's office on the *Excelsior* was precisely what you'd expect from one of the wealthiest men on the planet. His dark mahogany, gold-trimmed desk had once belonged to an eighteenth-century Indian Maharaja. On the walls hung priceless paintings, many of them originals by the Old Masters. At his feet lay the finest Persian rugs. The only items which stood in contrast to Khan's image as a modern-day robber baron were the row of picture frames lined up on the windowsill behind him. Holographic portraits were the norm, but for Khan, there was something to be said for an object you could grasp in your hands.

Those sacred images had been taken in his younger, more idealistic days. The summer of '22 he'd spent working for Greenpeace, hounding whaling ships from inflatable dinghies. Beside that stood another image from two years later when he'd built homes in Peru with Habitat for Humanity. Each image featured a cherished moment now frozen in time. So near and yet in many ways they were from another life.

Khan often reflected on his radical past during the mind-numbing reams of paperwork he had to approve on a daily basis. With the flick of his finger, he scrolled through three-dimensional holographic documents suspended in midair before him.

"Confirm," he murmured to the voice recognition software every few seconds, whereby a beam of light from the document would attach his retinal signature.

During interviews, Khan was often asked by the media how he was able to reconcile a past spent fighting global corporate interests with becoming one himself. They expected him to disown his past, ask for forgiveness, as though he owed them an explanation for his sudden about-face. In the end, neither assumption was even close to the truth. Khan had never run from his past. Far from it—he'd gladly brought many of these hard-won lessons with him into the corporate world. Tough battles waged in courts as well as out in the open had left him callused in the way only war could.

As Dr. Erwin had pointed out, following his father's death, his mother had pleaded that he return home and save the family steel business from bankruptcy. It hadn't been an easy decision. In many ways the company had represented everything Khan had rebelled against. And yet the responsibility to family had proven stronger. Before long, Khan had been forced to put aside the altruism that ran so powerfully through his veins so he might bring to bear every dirty trick he'd learned up to that point.

Now those pictures were all that remained of that alter ego. Once in a while, Khan looked back with derision at his naivety. Other times, he longed for a return to that period when his life had held at least a semblance of purpose.

The clock by the muted television monitor read sixty-eight hours and nine minutes. That was how long Vacek and the others had left to complete their mission before the virus became too widespread to be stopped. On TV, a masked reporter stood before throngs of people lined up to get gas. More unsettling images in front of grocery stores and pharmacies followed. The world was on the brink. Within the next few days, the delicate seams of civilization would begin to crumble. After that, all hope would be lost.

A buzz from the sleek audio unit on his desk snapped him from his reverie. It was his secretary and he pushed the button to respond.

"What is it?"

"Ms. Meadows to see you," his secretary told him.

"Fine. Send her in."

The stout mahogany double doors swung open on their own as Meadows entered, her head held high, her lips tight. Khan knew that expression well and it normally signaled the approach of bad news. Meadows was flanked by two men in white lab coats.

"All right," Khan said. "Out with it."

The first lab technician had short scruffy hair and barely looked a day over twenty-three. His hands were trembling.

"Those temporal fluctuations we recorded forty-eight hours ago…"

"Yes," Khan snapped impatiently. "What about them?"

The second technician stepped forward. She was a petite European female. Thankfully for her, she was far more pleasant to look at than her bumbling colleague. "They just spiked, sir."

Her accent was from somewhere in Northern Italy, but Khan couldn't place it right away.

He drew in a slow breath to help maintain his composure. "By how much?"

"Off the charts," Meadows said, stepping into the conversation.

Pressing his lip against his lower teeth, Khan said, "What do you make of it?"

The Italian technician started in with the mumbo-jumbo right away. "Clearly temporal integrity is being compromised, sir. It's approaching critical mass. I suggest—"

Khan slammed his fist against the desk, causing those before him to flinch. "I pay these people an arm and a leg," he complained, eyeing Meadows. "And not one of them can speak plain English." There was more than a touch of menace in his tone and it wasn't lost on those present.

"It's the target," Meadows explained in simple terms. "Lacroix?"

She nodded. "Yes. He's making alterations."

A single bead of sweat betrayed Khan's steely confidence. He reached into a side drawer of his desk without finding what he was searching for. Stopping, he said, "What you're telling me is that he's changing the past."

"Yes."

He continued rifling through his desk, growing more and more agitated as the object of his search continued to elude him. "So what can we do about it?"

Meadows poured herself a glass of water and drank half of it, perhaps sensing what was about to come. "Right now, Mr. Khan, there isn't much we can do, I'm afraid, apart from pray that the latest team does what they're supposed to."

"Dammit," Khan swore and tapped hard against the red button on his desk.

"Yes, Mr. Khan," came his secretary's serene reply.

"Shirley, the goddamn Hennessy isn't in my desk. I had two bottles and now there isn't a single one."

"I'm sorry, sir, I don't know anything about it. But I'll have the cleaning staff terminated at once."

"You do that. Oh, and Shirley, get me a glass of something—and make sure it's strong."

Chapter 16

The cooking fires in the village continued to smolder even though there was no one to tend to them. Anders crossed the open ground toward the large pit-house, picking up discarded items from each of their pillaged packs. His arms filled with MREs and three pairs of women's underwear, he stopped at the fire pit to inspect the skull the native women had been defleshing. It looked like the skull of a Neanderthal.

"I don't believe they were going to eat it," Khazanov said, standing off his left shoulder. He was resting as much of his weight as he could on a walking stick.

"The thought did cross my mind," Anders admitted.

"Removing the flesh had more to do with preparing the skull for some form of ancestor worship. The totem pole is filled with carvings of village elders." He waved his hand over his head. "I'll bet if we looked we'd find a shrine somewhere close, filled with bones."

Anders glanced around. Beyond the sound of birds cooing, the area was eerily silent. From there, Anders and

Khazanov walked to the main structure where they hoped to find the rest of their equipment.

"Any thoughts on what happened back there?" Anders asked. He was referring to the craft they'd seen capturing groups of natives.

Khazanov considered the question. "Vacek implied they were from another group, but I was under the impression that Genesis employees were the only ones from the future operating in this time period."

"That's what I thought." They entered the musty-smelling hut and spotted where the packs had been upended on the dusty ground. Several items remained in a pile. "At the very least, it suggests there's more going on here than we were told."

Just then, Vacek shoved past them and began rooting through the pile. "I'll bring everything out into the open so we can repack this mess and get moving."

"Won't it go faster if we work together?" Anders suggested.

"Don't worry," Vacek told him flatly. "I got it. Just keep an eye out along the perimeter in case those savages decide to come back and finish off what they started."

Reluctantly, Anders and Khazanov turned and left. Once outside, they found Riese studying the skull.

"Fascinating, isn't it?" she said.

Anders shrugged. "It seems the mystery behind the Neanderthal extinction wasn't nearly as dramatic as we eggheads imagined it to be all these years," Anders replied, still clutching the MREs and undergarments. "I think it's safe to say they weren't chased out of their environment by *Homo sapiens*, but rather assimilated through breeding."

Riese laughed. "Are you always so full of yourself?"

Anders shrugged.

"Whoever this skull belonged to," she continued, "died a very unpleasant death."

83

"What do you mean?" Khazanov asked.

Using a stick, Riese rotated the skull. "Look at the lesions on the frontal bone. There are only a handful of viral diseases known to cause those kinds of marks. At the top of that list is venereal syphilis."

Anders' face squished up. "Are you saying our dead guy here was a player who stuck it in the wrong primate?"

Khazanov exploded with laughter.

"I can't tell if this was a male or female," Riese said, her face flushed with anger. "But I can tell you syphilis wasn't known to exist this far back."

"Perhaps it was brought back by someone from the future," Anders theorized.

Riese shook her head. "I doubt it. The disease has largely been eradicated."

"Could it be a case of Pyric Hemorrhagic Fever?"

She grew quiet, her face showing concern as she stood, her eyes passing over the items in Anders' hands. "Hey, those are mine," she shouted, clutching at the pink frilly underwear.

Anders didn't resist. "I was actually coming to speak with you about those," he said. "Help me understand this. You get the once-in-a-lifetime opportunity to travel back thousands of years and you bring sexy panties? Who exactly did you think you were going to meet?"

Riese snatched the final pair and gave Anders a hard shove. He stumbled back and nearly fell over.

"What I wear under my clothes is none of your business—not anymore, at least."

Vacek emerged a second later, wearing his pack and carrying several more. They'd all been restocked. "I replaced things as best I could. Of course, I can't promise everything is back where it should be, but that's something we can worry about later tonight when we make camp. For now, we need to get moving before we lose any more daylight." He brought the OLED display to his lips. "Stills, Halloway, Castleman. Fold in the perimeter and prepare to move out."

"Roger that," came three quick replies.

"All right, people, let's move," Vacek barked, sounding more like a drill sergeant than the head of a security detail. "We need to put as much distance between us and this village as possible." He wiped the beads of sweat off his forehead and glanced up at the sun.

"How many hours before dark, you think?" Anders asked.

Vacek winced. "Not nearly enough."

Chapter 17

The humidity in the air was nearly suffocating as the group set out from the village. Vacek, a skilled tracker, took point. If they were in Neolithic North Africa, as Khazanov had assured them they were, then the island laboratory they were searching for lay somewhere to the northwest. Short of flying there in a Cutter, they had little choice but to trek through the thick jungle in that direction.

Cutting through the heavy brush, Anders couldn't help wondering about the raid against the village they'd witnessed and Vacek's insistence they keep out of view from the passing ship. It wasn't clear yet what was behind his rather peculiar reaction. Had a rival corporate faction somehow founded their own competing settlement in the past or was there something else afoot? Either way, it was clear the team of scientists had been fed only half the story.

A brief conversation with Binh had made clear that his friend, normally an excellent judge of character, agreed. They hadn't simply gotten off on the wrong foot. Something about this mission just wasn't right.

The group was less than thirty minutes from the village when they came upon Vacek kneeling by the forest floor, examining a disturbance in the underbrush.

"What is it, boss?" Stills asked, swiping a layer of sweat off his shaved head and flicking it to the ground.

Vacek pointed to a pair of footprints. "One set of tracks. Bipedal humanoid. Very large."

"Maybe it's one of the escaping villagers," Erwin said, hopeful.

"Not unless he wears a size twenty-five," Vacek countered as he plucked hairs from the footprint and sniffed them. "It's a primate."

"Gorillas didn't live in these parts," Khazanov said as he moved in to inspect the tracks. He was an anthropologist as well as a linguist and this was his area of expertise.

"That's not the kind of primate I'm talking about," Vacek replied. "This thing is large enough to make a gorilla look like a spider monkey."

A dark cloud passed over Khazanov's face.

Riese cupped her elbows and scanned the hazy jungle. She was shivering in spite of the overpowering heat.

At once, Vacek's ears perked up. "You hear that?"

Erwin whimpered and clutched at Binh, who slapped him away.

Anders' hand came up holding his inhibitor. He strained to listen, focused on detecting the sound of nearby movement through the forest. Was something stalking toward them? "All I hear is water," Anders said at last.

Vacek's gaze settled on Anders. "That's right. There's a river not far from here. If we're lucky, it might take us to the coast."

Halloway and Stills went into their packs and came out with compact rifles, neatly folded in two. Snapping them open, they inserted fresh magazines. "A little extra firepower never hurt anyone," the medic said, grinning proudly.

Vacek motioned to both men. "Halloway, I want you and Stills to cut north and reconnoiter for that river. Check the shoreline for anything we can use as a raft." His voice lowered by three octaves. "And for God's sake, stay on your toes."

Stills' eyes slanted down to his rifle and then back to Vacek as if to say, *Who do you think you're talking to?*

"Just keep us posted," Vacek told him.

"Roger that," Stills replied. He and Halloway disappeared into the dense foliage.

Anders stood scanning the dark patches of jungle around them. Binh appeared beside him, sporting a rather serious expression, and spoke.

"I feel the same way," Anders conceded. "We're being watched."

•••

Trekking through the dense vegetation in the oppressive heat was slow going. Added to that was Erwin's constant need for bathroom breaks every twenty minutes. When he asked for the third time, Anders was just about ready to leave him behind. The paleobotanist undid his fly and was preparing to shuffle a few feet off the path when Khazanov ordered him to stop.

"Oh, goodness, what is it?" Erwin asked, his hands instinctively jumping above his head.

88

"Don't move an inch," the Russian said, dropping to one knee beside him. Khazanov then set his backpack down and removed an instrument with a pistol grip on one end and a scooper on the other.

"I appreciate the concern," Erwin said. "But I just had a prostate exam last week."

Binh burst out laughing.

Anders turned back, his nose twitching at the hint of a foul odor. "Khazanov, whatever this is, surely it can wait."

"No, this is important," Khazanov insisted and brushed aside leaves covering a large mound of feces.

Anders recoiled, covering his nose. "It's just a turd," he said.

"If we stop to inspect every dump we come across," Erwin said, "we won't get very far."

Khazanov dipped the scooper instrument into the feces and pulled the trigger. At once the collector retracted into the main body of the handheld machine. Lights next to a small display screen began to blink.

"What exactly are you doing?" Erwin asked, looking visibly strained from holding in his business.

"Back at the University of St Petersburg, I taught a class on the study of paleofeces."

Binh came alongside them and asked the obvious question.

"It's the study of excrement," Anders explained. "You can learn a lot about a man that way. With any luck, the device should provide him with a full DNA profile."

Their interest piqued, Vacek and Riese were now also hovering over Khazanov.

"In your case, Anders," Riese said, "future generations will dig you up and discover that some men are more full of shit than others."

Anders grinned. A tropical bird chirped out in the distance. He scanned the area around them. When his attention returned to Khazanov, the results were already in.

"How can that be?" Khazanov exclaimed.

The others around them grew increasingly nervous. A few feet away, Castleman stood guard, making sure no one or nothing came out at them from the jungle.

"What is it?" Erwin asked, growing more terrified by the second.

Anders glanced over Khazanov's shoulder at the name on the readout. "*Gigantopithecus*," he read aloud. "Didn't they go extinct three hundred thousand years ago?"

Looking down at the fresh clump of feces, Riese said, "Apparently not."

"We've been wrong before," Khazanov said. "Look at the Neanderthals we came across. It's really not surprising that few fossils have been found in this area. With sand dunes for thousands of miles, where would you even start? I tell you, moments like this are the reason I joined the expedition. You keep yourself locked in a museum basement long enough and you're liable to become an artifact yourself."

"Some gorilla took a dump," Erwin said with derision. He was behind a large leaf, finally relieving himself. "I guess I don't see the big deal."

Khazanov licked his lips, dried and cracking. "Try to picture a Sasquatch except much, much larger. The Gigantopithecus weighs over a thousand pounds, is covered in long fur and is highly territorial."

Putting on a brave face, Anders said, "Sounds a bit like Riese, if you ask me."

"Very funny," the Russian said. "But we need to leave this area as soon as possible." His eyes met Vacek. "You better warn your men."

Without wasting another second, Vacek flicked a switch and spoke into the OLED display on his wrist.

Castleman removed the magazine from his rifle and popped in another he'd retrieved from his pack. "If this thing's as big as you say, we're gonna need detonation rounds."

"Wait a minute. You can't kill it," Riese protested, mortified at the very thought. She appealed to Vacek for help. "Need I remind you we're in a very different world than the one back home? There are people and creatures walking about that haven't been seen for thousands of years. We can't very well start blasting everything that gives us the willies."

"That might be so," Castleman said. "But I see any damned thing like what he just described, I ain't gonna wait around to see if it's friendly. I'm gonna blow it another ten thousand years into the past."

Vacek was still fiddling with the OLED, his voice becoming more desperate. "Bird one to bird two, come in. Bird one to bird two, come in."

The radio crackled with static. Binh spoke to Anders in Boatese.

"Binh's right," Anders said, addressing the others. "We need to head for the river and link up with Stills and Halloway. If we hurry, we can get there before King Kong shows up."

The group began to move, Vacek in the lead, followed by Anders, Binh and the others. Bringing up the rear was Castleman.

They hadn't gotten further than a few meters before Erwin came scrambling out of the brush and up the path behind them, buttoning his pants and cursing them for leaving him behind.

Anders grinned. Maybe now he would learn to hold it in.

Chapter 18

Several hours passed as the group searched for the river. More than once during that time they stopped while Vacek tried unsuccessfully to reach Stills and Halloway over the radio.

Binh lifted his canteen to his lips to shake out the last few drops. Pointing to a fallen tree they'd seen before, he rattled a few choice words off to Anders in Boatese.

Anders' soaking coveralls were practically glued to his skin. "I think Binh is right, we've already come this way," Anders said, taking a closer look as they trudged past a familiar rock. "Vacek, I'm getting the distinct impression we're heading in circles. I'm running out of faith that you know where the hell you're leading us."

"We're waiting on word from the advance party," Castleman responded, sounding more than a little curt. Everyone's water and energy was starting to run low, along with their patience.

"What makes you think Stills and Halloway aren't just as lost as we are?" Riese asked. "I thought Vacek was supposed to be some kind of kickass tracker."

"I work better at night," Vacek said. "Navigating by the stars."

Anders chuckled, pulling his sticky clothes away from his chest. "You do realize this far back in the past, the night's sky isn't the same."

"Do you take me for an idiot?" the lead mercenary barked. "As part of my mission prep, I studied star placement from the tenth millennium BCE. I could survive out here for a month with nothing more than a hunting knife. What about you?"

Anders didn't bother responding to that one. Everyone's nerves were beyond frayed. A pissing contest would only cause more problems than they needed right now.

Riese stopped before a giant leaf and watched as a trickle of water rolled along its smooth surface and dripped onto the jungle floor. She reached out with the clear intention of tilting the droplets into her mouth when Erwin shouted at her to stop.

Riese paused and threw him a look of annoyance. "You better have a damn good reason for raising your voice," she warned him.

"Ancient philodendrons," Erwin told her, indicating the plant she'd been about to grab. "Very poisonous. You drink that water and within two minutes your tongue'll swell to the size of a balloon. Within three you'll suffocate to death."

Riese let the water spill to the ground, watching it splatter on a dead leaf.

Anders patted Erwin's shoulder. "She's got problems saying thank you."

The sound of snapping twigs and rustling leaves up ahead drew everyone's attention. Vacek raised an arm, his fingers clenched into a tight fist, signaling for the group to halt and keep quiet. Anders removed his weapon, his pulse quickening as his vision struggled to penetrate the thick jungle around them. The noise of rustling trees and bushes turned into grunting as Castleman appeared before them, holding a child with a white-painted face who was dressed in animal skins. The kid spun in an attempt to free himself and nearly got away, but Castleman was too fast and held him in a bear hug, lifting him off the ground. The child's legs kicked at empty air.

After a moment of fruitless struggle, he relaxed and Castleman deposited him on his feet. The kid had dirty blond hair and striking blue eyes. He was still wearing the necklace with his mother's tooth and lock of hair. But he'd also added the arm patch Anders had given him to the trinkets around his neck. Anders recognized him right away as the hybrid child named Aku they'd seen in the camp, the one who'd poked at him playfully through the bars of their wooden prison.

"He's been following us since we left the village," Vacek said. "I stumbled onto his tracks shortly after we discovered the marks left by Khazanov's giant primate friend."

The child spotted Anders and a smile grew on his lips.

Riese wheeled about with a look of astonishment.

The archaeologist threw up his hands. "What can I say, I have an effect on people."

"You sure do," she replied.

"We should have hit the river by now," Vacek cut in. "Khazanov, see if the boy can tell us how to get there."

The Russian limped forward. "I'll do my best." Khazanov uttered a few words in that strange language.

As he spoke, his hands mimicked the movement of a boat, floating on water. Almost on cue, the half-Neanderthal child giggled and began to speak, parroting Khazanov's hand gestures.

"I'm not sure I'm getting this right," Khazanov said. "He's saying something about a tall white man who lives by the river."

The muscles in Vacek's formidable jaw clenched. "Tell   him   to   take   us   to   him."

•••

Dusk was fast approaching as Aku led them down a slope and into a shallow valley where the sound of rushing water became stronger. Hearing it, the group pressed on, eager to find the man Aku had spoken of before darkness fell.

Not long after that, they spotted the river and a small enclosure nestled by the water's edge. A crude-looking wooden palisade twenty feet in diameter surrounded a simple shack. The high walls were braced with bits of scavenged metal and the top was ringed with razor wire. Whoever this man was, he was eager to keep someone, or something, out.

Vacek and Castleman kept their rifles in the low ready position as the group drew closer.

A man in orange coveralls came into view, seated in a handmade wooden chair at the water's edge. He was carving out the trunk of a tree. Standing behind to him were Stills and Halloway.

Anders was relieved to see they were still alive. Vacek thought differently.

"Give me one good reason why I shouldn't gut the two of you right here and now," the mercenary leader said, his palm resting on the handle of his combat knife.

The man in the coveralls stood and extended his hand to Vacek. He was thin, if not a little disheveled, with pleasant features and salt-and-pepper hair. His skin was leathery, his eyes fatigued. He had the weathered look of a man who'd spent far too much time alone in the bush.

"Sam Grieves," he said, finishing the shake and then fixing his orange coveralls. "It's not their fault, Chief. Their comm link must have shorted when they fell into the river."

Vacek wasn't having any of it. "You know, if it wasn't for Aku…" he said, searching around and realizing the boy had disappeared again. His gaze settled back on Grieves, his voice dropping to a more soothing, diplomatic tone. "We're looking for a boat to bring us downriver."

"Your men have already asked me, kemosabe," Grieves said, setting the adze against the palisade wall. An axe-like instrument with a curved blade to carve wood, the adze dated back to the Stone Age. "And I'll tell you the same thing I told them, it's out of the question. I only got the one boat. Besides"—he nodded his head at the setting sun—"what you folks need more than a boat is a safe place to lay your heads tonight. Believe me when I say you don't wanna be out there when it gets dark."

Chapter 19

Night fell and the jungle settled into a steady rhythm of nocturnal sounds. Insects, birds, frogs, each sang in mating rituals that dated back millions of years. The noises made Anders thankful for the walls that surrounded them, shoddy-looking as they were.

All ten of them, Grieves included, sat around a meager fire. Their host, his fingers chipped and scarred from a lifestyle which eschewed luxury, held a gutted lizard impaled on the end of a branch over the fire. The flesh crackled and popped and Anders had to admit the smell wasn't half bad. Grieves pulled it out of the flames, offering the first taste to Riese, who shook her head with only a partial attempt to hide her disgust. She'd decided to eat a granola bar from one of her few remaining MREs instead. Although they had managed to retrieve most of the items stolen from their packs after the natives had gone through their belongings, several of the MREs had never been found. Vacek had been the one to reorganize what was left of the equipment and it was beginning to look as though he'd distributed the bulk of the remaining food to him and his men.

It was also becoming increasingly clear that Vacek saw Anders and the other scientists as impediments to their mission of rendezvousing with the stranded colony and returning with the vaccine.

Grieves passed the crisp lizard down the line from person to person until he reached Binh, who snatched the critter and devoured it gladly.

Anders asked his friend how it tasted and Binh became thoughtful, replying that it tasted like lizard. The response brought a smile to Anders' face and made perfect sense since the Vietnamese tended to eat just about anything they could get their hands on. He'd read somewhere it was a carryover from the twentieth-century war with the United States. Suffering under heavy American bombardment, the North Vietnamese had often been forced to eat anything they found in the jungle. Meals of pork or chicken had been replaced with spiders and cockroaches.

Anders watched as the flames from the fire danced hypnotically.

"I'm guessing Genesis sent you back," Grieves said. He skewered another lizard and held it over the fire.

Binh watched with delight, licking his fingers.

"That's one way of putting it," Anders replied. "They dumped us into a lake two hundred feet from a group of cannibals."

Grieves grinned, his hair looking mostly gray in the firelight. "The Neanderthals don't much trust our kind, and who can blame 'em. I mostly keep to myself out here, which is probably why they pretty much leave me alone."

Khazanov spooned a healthy portion of chicken primavera from his MRE into his mouth, leaving a creamy trail on the edges of his beard. "One of them is half Neanderthal and half *sapiens*."

"That may be," Vacek replied. "But it makes no difference to our mission. They're savages and I don't trust 'em as far as I can throw 'em. I've heard stories from men who've been sent back to this godforsaken place. Stories that would make your skin crawl. Neanderthals hunting grown men as though they were animals, skinning them alive, plucking their beating hearts from their chests. Let me tell you, they'll slit your throat and eat your spleen without batting an eyelid."

Grieves laughed and Vacek's head snapped in his direction.

"They're a superstitious and primitive people," Grieves said. "No doubt about that. The white powder they put on their skin—they think it makes 'em look like us. When I first arrived I was scared too, but that was mostly because of what I'd been told beforehand by the corporate culture at Genesis. Neanderthals are far from a band of hippies, but that doesn't make them monsters, at least not the way the company would have us believe."

Anders thought at once about how Aku had led them to Grieves. "I noticed one of the women in camp was using a Bowie knife."

"We trade sometimes," Grieves explained. "They gather a wild grain and refine it into a kind of powder."

"You're talking about millet flour," Erwin said, stabbing the fire with a stick. "Comes from the eleusine coracana plant and makes a dish some Africans call Ugali."

"That's right," Grieves said, looking a little put out. "Add a little boiled water and work it with a wooden spoon for twenty minutes and you've got yourself a great simple meal. It's taken some time, but the natives have learned to trust me."

"So much for trust after what we saw today," Vacek said and spat into the flames.

Grieves looked puzzled.

"We were there when a ship came and snatched up a bunch of them," Riese explained. "Nearly got us too."

"Lacroix's men," Grieves said. "They use 'em as pack animals. Manual labor. One of the many reasons I left those assholes. Primitive as they may be, that ain't right. And some of the shit the corporation was doing…" He trailed off. "Hell, I prefer to take my chances out here."

A shrill cry emanated from the darkness beyond the walls. Even the mercenaries couldn't hide the alarm that had slithered into their hearts.

"The heck was that?" Erwin demanded, peering over his shoulder.

Suddenly the wooden palisade seemed weak and terribly inadequate.

"Oh, that," Grieves said.

"We saw *Gigantopithecus* tracks not far from here," Riese told him.

Grieves poked the fire with a stick. "That's one name for 'em, I suppose. I call 'em the boss of the woods."

"One set of tracks we found belonged to a real big bastard," Vacek said.

Nodding, Grieves said, "They're fairly peaceful, unless you go and do something stupid to piss 'em off."

Khazanov's hand had settled over the wound on his leg, wincing from the apparent pain. "You ever pissed one off?" the Russian asked.

Grieves laughed. "I'm alive, aren't I?"

"Hey, big man, you sure you're all right?" Anders asked Khazanov.

"Fit as a fiddle," the Russian lied, clearly doing his best to swallow the pain.

100

Almost on cue, Halloway got up and went over to check on him. Halloway had already bandaged him up in the village, but that was hours ago. "Let me have another look at that wound."

After several attempts to fend the medic off, the proud Khazanov finally relented.

With his friend being cared for, Anders shifted his attention back to Grieves.

"Two things we need to know. Where we are and how we get to the island laboratory."

"You mean Gihon?" Grieves nodded at Vacek. "Your gruff friend over there has the right idea. The river should lead you into the Atlantic. From there you can hitch a ride on a local fishing boat. They're more than familiar with foreigners dressed in strange clothing. By now the only ones who see us as gods are those living in the bush."

"Seems the colony isn't afraid of interacting with the locals," Riese observed.

Grieves fished a cigarette from his pocket and lit it. "You don't know the half of it." He offered one to the others, but only Vacek and Binh accepted. Grieves motioned to the four scientists. "I'll be honest. You folks don't look to me like the usual Genesis types I've seen around these parts."

"I'll take that as a compliment," Anders said under his breath.

"You might say we're on contract," Erwin told him.

"A pandemic has broken out back home," Riese explained, except 'home' in this context meant a present that was rapidly becoming inhospitable. "We've come back to link up with the colony and collect a vaccine."

The weathered features on Grieves' shifted into something resembling concern. "About a week ago I came across a man in a jumpsuit north of here. His right

101

ankle was sprained pretty badly. I did what I could to help him and the darnedest thing happened."

"What's that?" Anders asked, indulging him.

Grieves looked up at him. "He told me the same story you're telling me now."

Anders' surprise at the news was drowned out by Khazanov's shriek of pain.

"I was afraid of that," Halloway said, looking concerned. He'd removed the bandage and pressed slightly on the wound only to see pus squirt out. "His leg's infected. Anders, in my pack there's a medical kit. Can you grab it for me?"

"Sure, if you think you can help him," Anders said, pulling a pen light from his pocket and heading for Grieves' hut. All of their packs were in a corner, stacked like cordwood. Anders stopped for a moment, trying to remember which one belonged to Halloway. He opened two of them and jabbed his hand inside without finding anything useful. He was about to open the third when Vacek appeared.

"What are you doing?"

Anders twisted around. "Is there a problem?"

Vacek rubbed the edges of his goatee. He brushed past Anders and reached for Halloway's pack. The tattoo on his arm looked like something he'd gotten in the army. The two men exchanged a tense look.

"See, I got it," Vacek said, bumping shoulders as he left.

Anders returned to the fire, more concerned for Khazanov than confused over Vacek's strange behavior. Halloway opened the bag and fished out his medical kit. What the Russian needed was fresh bandages and some antibiotics. And what he needed even more was a well-equipped hospital. Knowing Khazanov, a gaggle of attractive nurses wouldn't hurt either.

At last, Anders' focus returned to Vacek, who was sitting by the fire, his pack between his legs, staring in the dancing flames. Whatever was in that pack, it was something he hadn't wanted Anders to see.

Chapter 20

Epsilon Cloister House, 2059
One week after the outbreak

The monk entered the Epsilon Cloister House both excited and fearful. Ever since his entry into the brotherhood, Father Yohann had been there to keep him surefooted and steadfast on the path to righteousness.

Normally that meant a firm word or two on rare occasions when his faith had faltered. Sometimes, those words had turned to physical violence, abuse the monk had never experienced in his old life. He'd grown up in a loving home with parents who wanted only the best for him. They'd taught him the deep value of human life as well as a commitment to a higher learning. The beatings he had received at the monastery, infrequent as they were, had ignited in him a burning desire to lash out and strike back. And yet to give in to those urges would only prove he had learned nothing.

He was here to master the flesh, not have it master him.

The monk entered a long dark corridor and soon came to a set of heavy wooden doors. He pulled them open and let himself inside, his sandals scraping along the cold stone floor. By contrast to the hallway, the ceremonial room was warmly lit by two rows of candles perched on golden stands. Centering the room was a circular depression that featured the symbol for which they'd been named: five overlapping circles, one for each of the world's five major religions—although the monk liked to think of those rings as representing the four cardinal points, with the last to bind them all together. Thesis, antithesis and synthesis.

Nearly forty years before, the Pope at the time, Francis, had called on the followers of Christianity, Islam, Judaism, Buddhism, and Hinduism to set aside their long-standing disputes.

Back then, the planet had been gripped by zealotry. Faith-based conflicts were increasing at an alarming rate. The Pope's appeal had been for the creation of a neutral body to help mediate disputes and unite the major religions against what they believed was an even greater threat: the spread of atheism. The previous century had done much to see the advance of science and the ever-shrinking place for faith in the life of the average person.

Thus was born the Epsilon Brotherhood, a multi-faith organization tasked with running what was popularly referred to as the United Nations of religion. Muslim, Hindu, Christian… adherents of all faiths were welcome to join, so long as they made the cut. What one believed was less important than the individual's undying devotion to fulfill the organization's mandate, its sacred commitment to protect and preserve the faithful anytime and anywhere.

105

None of Epsilon's founding fathers could have imagined that a new and far more insidious threat would emerge in just a few short decades. When secret agents working for the Brotherhood began reporting that a company called Genesis had discovered three portals and that at least one of them led into the past, the implications weren't immediately clear. It was a doorway, the agents had explained, leading to somewhere in the eleventh century BCE.

The elders agreed that the universe was indeed a mysterious and splendid creation. And yet their initial ambivalence turned to deep concern when a disturbing possibility began to emerge. If the proverbial flapping of a butterfly's wings could cause hurricanes on the other side of the world, then what sacred aspects of our present might be altered by men and women sent into the past? Might Jesus, Buddha and Mohammed blink out of history on account of a single careless act? The possibilities were suddenly more than terrifying, they were unacceptable. Something needed to be done. Each of the portals needed to be closed, beginning with the third and most dangerous.

Father Yohann sat at an ornate table within the circular depression. He waved the monk over, inviting him to join him.

"Your many years of training are nearly at an end," Yohann said, his voice echoing in the vast, empty chamber. "There is but one test which remains." And with that Yohann pushed a manila folder across the table's smooth surface.

The monk peeled open the cover. Inside were dossiers on half a dozen individuals, many of them academics and professors in fields ranging from archaeology and anthropology to geology and botany. Apart from standard biodata, the files contained the most recent intelligence on each subject's last known location.

"We've received news that Genesis is assembling a team to reclaim their lost biofacility and I'm afraid we can't allow that to happen."

The monk flipped through the files and settled on the last one.

Dr. Gustave Hiddenger
Location: Prague, Czech Republic
Age: 59
Occupation: Archaeologist

"Your first objective is to eliminate each of the targets," Father Yohann told him.

The image associated with Hiddenger's file showed an overweight man who drank too much and looked years past his prime. An easy and enjoyable target. The monk would save him for last.

"Once that part of your mission is completed," Yohann went on, "the final phase of the operation can begin."

The monk didn't flinch. He'd been trained extensively in covert action—intelligence-gathering and counterintelligence as well as assassination. Besides, he'd had plenty of practice. Over the last decade, Genesis had become the Brotherhood's number one foe and month after month the monk's list of sensitive assignments seemed to grow exponentially.

Father Yohann's suggestion that he would be involved in the final phase of the operation piqued the monk's interest. "Are there any details you can reveal ahead of time?" he asked, certain he wouldn't get much, but willing to try nevertheless.

Yohann grinned and patted the monk's rough hand. "You only get dessert once you finish the main meal. But I can tell you it will undoubtedly solve our current conflict with Genesis once and for all."

107

The monk collected the folder and the two men stood, the monk nearly a foot taller than his spiritual mentor.

"Our chances of success…" the monk began as he prepared to leave. "How good are they?"

A paternal smile formed on Yohann's lips. "With five gods standing behind you, how could you possibly fail?"

Chapter 21

70 hours remaining

Riese emerged from the shack early the next morning and stretched, enjoying the early morning stillness. Most of the others, Anders and Binh included, had slept by the fire. Like a true gentleman, Grieves had offered up his bunk inside to Khazanov, who now limped out behind Riese with noticeable difficulty.

"A shot of vodka would do me well," the Russian lamented.

Binh seconded that motion with great enthusiasm.

"My head's still hurting from the Hennessy we drank on the *Excelsior*," Anders said, rising to his feet.

"I won't lie," Riese said, setting her pack against the palisade and taking a seat by the fire. "I'm so hungry right now I could eat a cow."

Grieves held up six lizard kebabs he'd been cooking over an open flame.

Riese's hand covered her mouth. "Oh, please no."

Nearby, Vacek and Castleman were busy cleaning their rifles. A towel was laid across a log seat next to them, littered with springs and other gun parts.

Erwin arrived with a cup of water he'd taken from the river in one hand and a toothbrush in the other. "Anyone seen Stills and Halloway?"

"Good question," Khazanov replied. "I was hoping for another shot of that sweet pain medication from last night."

"They went to gather more firewood," Vacek said, cleaning his weapon. "You do plan on eating breakfast, don't you?"

Foam around his mouth, Erwin froze. "What'd I say?"

The sound of excited voices drew everyone's attention. It was Stills and Halloway. They weren't even at the gate but they were already calling for the gate to be opened. For a moment, Anders felt a streak of fear flutter inside his belly. He and Binh exchanged a look of concern.

Grieves pulled open the gate. Both men came bounding in, Stills cradling what looked like a bipedal creature covered in long red fur.

"I am not shitting you," Stills exclaimed, out of breath. "This place keeps getting weirder. Dr. Khazanov, you're gonna have to settle a bet. Is this thing human or ape?"

Khazanov rose to his feet, suddenly oblivious to the pain in his leg. His lower jaw came unhinged. "Is that what I think it is?" Anders asked, his eyes locked on what looked like a young *Gigantopithecus*. Even at three feet tall, it probably wasn't more than an infant.

The lizard kebabs tumbled from Grieves' hands and into the fire. "Are you two insane? You can't bring that here. Where in God's name did you find it?"

"We were collecting firewood," Halloway said, still out of breath. "Saw this cute little bugger sitting on a log, staring up at us."

"You're gonna get us all killed," Grieves shouted. "Hurry the hell up and put it back where you found it." He was pacing back and forth now, clutching his forehead.

Stills, upset with the reproach, shook his head. "We weren't gonna hurt him. We knew none of you would believe us unless you saw it with your own eyes."

Vacek was making ready to stand up when Anders put a hand on his shoulder. "They weren't there yesterday when we found the tracks. How were they supposed to know?"

"Frankly, they shouldn't be touching a damn thing," Vacek shouted. Parts from his rifle fell onto the ground and became covered with dirt. "Now look what you made me do." He threw the towel aside and charged at his men, knocking Stills over. Halloway reeled back, tripping over a chair and flinging the baby *Gigantopithecus* to the ground. It rolled over twice and knocked its head on a piece of firewood. Dazed, it sat up before drawing in a deep breath.

"Oh, this is not going to end well," Anders said as the creature began to howl.

"Somebody shut that thing up," Erwin shouted, his mouth still lathered with toothpaste.

A deafening roar echoed through the forest and danced up Anders' spine. Then came the sound of huge, thundering footsteps stomping toward them. Then the sharp crack of trees snapping like twigs. Whatever was coming, it was big and, above all, it was angry.

"Close the gate!" Grieves yelled.

Stills and Vacek shut the gate and slid the wooden crossbar into place.

111

Anders went to the creature, sitting on the ground, wailing. "We gotta get this thing out of here," he told them, "before Mama busts down that door."

The sound of angry footfalls was growing louder every second.

A light went on behind Vacek's eyes and he sprang into action and lifted the door latch. But no sooner had he swung the gate open than he shut and bolted it straight away. "Holy shit, it's huge." The baby continued to howl as Vacek's panicked eyes caught Riese's. "Can't you do anything to shut it up?"

Riese's features were wrought with terror and shock at Vacek's request. "What do you want me to do, breastfeed it and read it a story?"

Binh cackled with laughter.

"You always wanted to see a *Gigantopithecus* up close and personal," Anders told Khazanov. "Looks like now's your chance."

A pair of massive, fur-covered hands clamped down on the top of the gate and shook it back and forth. The entire wall around them shuddered. Vacek and the others scrambled away from the gate. Tears began to form in Erwin's eyes along with a wet patch along the crotch of his coveralls.

"I don't wanna die," he chanted. "Not like this."

Anders pulled out his inhibitor and yanked Riese close to him, distinctly aware that she'd immediately clung to him.

Another violent shake from those furry hands was accompanied by the sound of splintering wood as the gate was ripped from its hinges. The creature tossed it some distance into the woods as the rest of the palisade collapsed around them.

Now the *Gigantopithecus* was fully visible and for a brief moment, all they could do was stare in awe. The creature stood at over ten feet tall, a thousand pounds of

112

lean, rippled muscle. With long and powerful arms and a pair of compact legs, it was a sight to behold.

"It's got breasts," Khazanov observed with fascination. Even in the face of imminent death he was always the scientist.

Erwin's hand cramped around his weapon.

Riese held up her hand. "Hold your fire."

The baby *Gigantopithecus* rose to its feet and waddled to its mother. She took it in her arms and flipped it over, looking for any signs of harm. She then set it down and roared at the stunned group, stepping forward in a primal show of dominance.

Erwin pulled out his neural inhibitor and fired. A blue energy pulse shot from his weapon, striking the mother square in the chest. She paused for a moment, her face contorted with pain before she slumped forward, crashing to the ground where she lay motionless.

"You asshole, you killed it," Riese shouted, breaking free from Anders' grip.

Erwin's gaze flitted between the weapon in his hand and the beast. He dropped the inhibitor and took a step back. "I didn't mean to," he squealed. "My finger, it just twitched." He held out his index finger as if to prove his point.

"She isn't dead," Vacek said to Erwin. "But you may be when she wakes up."

Already, the fingers on the creature's giant hands were beginning to move.

Grieves fished out a burning stick from the fire. "If you're gonna leave, you better do it now," he said. The words were no sooner out of his mouth than Riese gasped with fright.

Grieves looked up to see the *Gigantopithecus* standing before him. He fought to swallow, his throat making an

113

audible clicking sound as the others grabbed what gear they could and broke for the carved canoe on the shoreline.

Desperately waving the fire stick back and forth, Grieves struggled to keep the creature at bay. A hopeful look appeared on Grieves' face. He was about to turn and hop in the boat when the flame flickered and then went out. The creature noticed it too and flicked the stick out of his hand, where it landed in the river with a sizzle. Then, with dizzying speed, she grabbed Grieves by the right arm and flung him like a child's toy. There was a crunch as Grieves' body smashed against a nearby Okoume tree.

With packs on, the group piled into the canoe and strained to paddle away from shore, some even using their hands to make the boat go faster.

They were only a few meters from shore when the *Gigantopithecus* waded into the river, water lashing against her lower torso, as she gave chase. Anders wasn't sure if he'd have more than one shot with his inhibitor and didn't dare risk firing until the beast drew closer. A few strokes later, the river's current took hold and whisked them away.

After nearly thirty minutes of hard paddling, they finally eased up.

Stills and Halloway were noticeably quiet, probably concerned what Vacek might do to punish them. But the paleobotanist deserved his own dose of the blame.

"When we get to shore," Anders told Erwin, "remind me to beat the crap out of you."

"It wasn't my fault," he pleaded. "I thought she was about to attack us."

114

"She was posturing," Riese corrected him. "She was only trying to protect her child. That was until you made it personal."

"What about Grieves?" Khazanov asked.

They'd been so panicked with the task of getting the canoe into deep water, they hadn't seen him get up after smacking into the side of that tree.

"He didn't make it," Vacek said coldly.

Anders drew in a deep breath. Even this early in the morning, the heat and humidity hung in the air like a dense fog.

Binh waved a hand to get Anders' attention and then cupped his ear. Anders listened. "I really hope you're wrong," he told Binh.

"What is it?" Vacek asked, clearly not in the mood for any more surprises. "We've already lost a good portion of our gear and weaponry."

"We may be about to lose a lot more than that," Anders replied.

Chapter 22

The water quickly grew choppy, the current too strong to head for shore. Anders called out for everyone to inflate their vests and hold on. There were only two paddles, one at the front with Vacek and the other in the rear with Anders. Both men cut through the water with everything they had. The powerful current swept the canoe along at high speed, spinning the boat around and knocking them into partially submerged rocks.

"Head for shore," Riese yelled, over the turbulence.

"Too late. The water's already got us," Anders shouted back. "Vacek, don't stop paddling."

They approached a dip where water flowed over an outcropping of boulders, forming a mini-waterfall. The front end rose and then quickly fell as they passed over the obstacle.

Binh whooped and waved his hands in the air.

"This isn't a damn concert," Anders chided him. "If you need something to do with your hands, put them in the water and paddle."

Then came another drop, this one larger than the last. The canoe splashed down and Anders yelped. "That's what I'm talking about."

Binh turned and gave him a dirty look.

After that the water settled a little. They'd navigated a rough patch and lived to tell about it. Anders was feeling proud, maybe even a little cocky.

He tapped Riese on the shoulder. "You stick with me and I'll get us home."

"I'll believe you when you can grow a pair of wings and fly us there."

Something over Riese's shoulder caught Anders' attention. An unusual motion in the water up ahead.

Twisting around, she caught sight of his worried gaze and spun to see a vortex of water churning not twenty feet away. A log floating in the river ahead of them got pulled in and sucked to the bottom before popping to the surface.

From the front of the canoe, Vacek began paddling madly to one side. Anders followed suit, hoping by some miracle they might evade the vortex by circling around it. But escaping its pull was like escaping a black hole. The canoe was heading right in and fast.

"Listen," Riese yelled to Anders. "Don't fight the water when it pulls you down or you'll drown."

He looked at her with saucer-shaped eyes.

Erwin overheard and swiveled too. "Let it swallow us? Riese, are you crazy?"

A second later, it had them. Their screams echoed against the surrounding jungle as the canoe was swallowed by the frothing whirlpool. Watery hands grabbed hold and yanked him to the bottom of the turbulent river, holding him there in spite of his inflatable vest. Seconds felt like hours as the oxygen in his lungs burned away. It took everything he had to follow Riese's advice and let the water take him. Just

117

when he was sure his lungs were about to explode, the river let go, sending Anders shooting to the surface, gasping for air. One by one, figures bobbed up around him, pushed along by the current and gradually deposited ashore, wet and battered. Not far away the canoe limped by, sporting a large hole and slowly sinking.

"That's just great," Erwin bitched to no one in particular. "That was our one chance to get back home and now it's gone."

Anders found Riese pulling herself onto a large rock and gave her a hand. She tried to resist at first, her pride kicking in, but quickly relented. "If it wasn't for you," he said, "I'd probably still be stuck underwater, fighting the current."

Wringing the water from her shirt, she said, "I suppose that's two you owe me then."

A few feet away, Stills stood watching the way Riese's wet clothes clung to her body, a lecherous expression on his face.

"If we ever get out of this mess," Anders promised, ignoring the merc's creepy stare, "I'll make it up to you."

"Don't count on it," she replied coolly. "You had your shot and you blew it." And with that she walked away without looking back.

Binh came up beside him looking like a drowned rat. A sheepish grin formed on his lips as he cupped an arm around Anders and offered a few words of tough love.

Anders shook his head. "Whose side are you on anyway?"

While the others took inventory of what had been lost, Castleman stomped out of the jungle, returning from a quick reconnaissance mission.

"We got something up ahead," he reported.

Vacek upended his boot and watched the water drain out. "How far away?"

"Few hundred yards, give or take," Castleman replied. He motioned to Khazanov. "Not sure what you wanna do about him though."

"He's the scientists' problem, not ours. They can carry him on their shoulders for all I care."

"Tell me we're not heading into another Neanderthal village," Halloway begged.

Castleman shook his head. "No, this is one of ours."

Chapter 23

On a good day covering three hundred yards in the jungle was difficult work. Doing so with a wounded man made it nearly impossible. Anders and Erwin were both tasked with acting like a pair of human crutches for the big Russian.

"You three better keep up or we're gonna leave you behind," Vacek said in the kind of cold, deep voice which made it clear that he meant every word.

They'd progressed perhaps two hundred yards inland from the river when Vacek pulled the column to a stop, patting his hand in the air for everyone to stay low and keep quiet.

Crouching, Anders made his way to the front. "What's the holdup?"

The merc leader was crouched, studying a muddy footprint in the soft earth. He picked up a few beige hairs and sniffed them.

"We're being stalked," he said, scanning from right to left.

Anders studied the footprint. It didn't resemble the one made by the *Gigantopithecus*. "Looks like a paw print."

Vacek spat, a trail of saliva running down his chin. "That's right. We got a cat on our tail and a big one."

Halloway shifted, looking wet and miserable. "The quicker we get where we're going, the better, I say."

When the canoe had capsized, the group had lost the remaining assault rifles along with most of the inhibitors and several of their packs.

"Hal's got a point," Castleman said. "No sense staying out in the open when God knows what is trailing us." Looking at Anders, he asked, "Your man, he gonna make it?"

"Oh, he's gonna make it," Anders assured him. Then to Vacek: "You move one of your team to the rear to watch our backs and we'll be just fine."

Vacek locked eyes with Stills and threw him a series of hand signals. The bald-headed merc swore and moved to the back of the line.

The group struggled on, stopping only once more to briefly rest. Anders unslung his pack and searched in vain for something substantial to eat. A few granola bars, some trail mix and a handful of crackers was all that was left.

"Vacek's hoarding the food," Anders said, certain that was the reason Vacek had been so eager to repack the bags himself.

He searched through Khazanov's belongings and found even less. Thankfully, each of them had been issued a water filtration bottle: a standard hardened plastic bottle with a built-in filter designed to keep even the smallest bacteria and viruses out. Halloway had joked that you could take a leak into the nozzle and end up with a decent-tasting glass of very warm water.

121

"I got a couple burritos if you want," Stills offered, tossing them over.

"Thank you," Anders replied, handing one to Khazanov.

"What about me?" Erwin asked, hand in the air like a kid who'd missed the candy bag.

Stills chuckled and threw him a packet of freeze-dried peanut butter and crackers.

"All this fancy food we brought with us isn't going to last," Anders noticed grimly. "We may need to start finding things to eat on our own."

Khazanov stifled a bout of laughter, squeezing his eyes shut instead to ward off the pain. "I doubt our path will lead us past any grocery stores," he said.

"I was thinking more about setting up traps," Anders responded. "We survived as a species for millennia without convenience stores and restaurants. There are more than a few tricks our ancestors could teach us."

Erwin slid his finger into the pouch of peanut butter and then into his mouth. "I seem to remember a paper you wrote on Neolithic hunting techniques?"

"Yes," Anders responded. "It was the subject of my graduate thesis and the reason Dr. Hiddenger asked me to accompany him to Anguillara Sabazia. They'd uncovered a Neolithic village at the bottom of a lake."

"God rest his soul," Khazanov said. "No man deserves to die like that."

Anders grew quiet. "What are you talking about?"

"You didn't hear?" Erwin stuttered, his mouth full of peanut butter.

"Hear what? My research vessel's spent the last few weeks out at sea. Why are you all looking at me like that?"

"I didn't want to be the one to tell you," Khazanov said, carefully. "But Dr. Hiddenger was killed. I heard it was a gas explosion of some kind."

122

Anders felt numb. The two men hadn't spoken in years and yet he'd always hoped that one day they'd mend the rift between them. "I can't believe it."

"Neither could we," Khazanov said with genuine compassion. "Especially when we heard it had happened after he'd been hired by Genesis."

Now Anders' head was really spinning.

"It was only after his death," Khazanov told him, "that they approached you to take his place."

Chapter 24

A short, difficult hike later they reached a perimeter fence. But this was no wooden palisade. Wooden posts placed every hundred feet bore rows of electric wire. Most of the cables were rusted, some even broken. Vines crawled up the posts in a signal of nature's slow, relentless advance.

"Is it electrified?" Vacek asked.

"Not anymore," Castleman told him.

Stills ran his hand up one particularly thick patch of vines working its way up a pole. Something was underneath it. He grabbed hold and tore the vine away to reveal a biohazard sign.

"Could this be it?" Erwin wondered, excited. "The lab we were sent back to check on."

"Keep your panties on, Erwina," Vacek snapped. "This is only one of several Genesis installations."

"Might be worth checking out anyway, Chief," Halloway suggested. "Yakov Smirnoff here ain't gonna make it much further on that bum leg of his."

"I don't want to hold anyone back," Khazanov said.

Vacek studied the way the Russian's leg was perched at an angle. "Then you better pray we find something that helps."

Past the perimeter fence they came upon a series of abandoned concrete structures. It was clear that at one point the facility had been well-manicured, but since then the ravages of time and weather had taken their toll.

There were five buildings in all. The living quarters, clinic and convalescence wings formed a U and made up the largest structures, while power and sanitation were tucked away behind the others. In the center was a dilapidated pergola with a concrete fountain underneath. The water inside was black and filled with dead leaves.

"I don't wanna stay here any longer than we need to," Vacek informed the others. "Let's break into three groups. Castleman and Erwin, take the living quarters. Stills, go with Anders, Binh and Riese to the clinic. Halloway and I will check out convalescence and the power station."

"What about me?" Khazanov asked.

"You wait here," Vacek said. "And if you see anything that means to kill us, give a holler."

Anders flicked on his pen light as they entered the damp and eerie confines of the clinic. Close behind were Binh, Riese and Stills. Mountains of medical debris littered the room. Rows of hospital beds, many of them flipped onto their side, lined both walls. The hollow sound of dripping water only added to their growing sense of disquiet.

"Whatever happened here," Anders said, "these folks sure left in a hurry." He kicked a bag of discarded surgery scrubs across the room, raising his arms for a successful field goal.

125

"Would you stop messing around?" Riese chided him. "Keep your eyes peeled for fresh bandages."

"I hate to break it to you, but we're more likely to find a fresh case of Dengue fever in this dump than anything that will help Khazanov."

"That's great to hear," Riese snapped. "So why don't you go ahead and run away, then? It's what you do best, isn't it?"

Anders grabbed a handful of discarded papers. "I got an idea, why don't we use these useless documents to make Khazanov a papier-mâché leg."

Stills snapped at them from the other end of the room, "You two find anything yet?"

"Course not," Anders said. "I told you this would be a giant waste of time. What we need to do is get Khazanov to Gihon and in front of a doctor as soon as possible."

A thick drop of water landed on Stills' bald head. He slapped it away with annoyance. "I'm gonna go check on your Russian friend. Meet me back there when you're done."

No sooner had Stills left than Anders began to wonder if he'd been too hard on Riese. He was still dealing with the painful news of Hiddenger's death. "Look," he said, prying open a box of medical supplies, "I'm not usually this big a jerk."

"This is a lot for all of us to take in," she began and then stopped short as her demeanor shifted. From out of a cabinet, Riese emerged with a roll of bandages still tightly wrapped in plastic. She tossed the package in the air and caught it. "Ye of little faith."

He smiled. "All right, congratulations. You were right and I was wrong. Happy now?"

"Hmm, getting there. Say it again."

But before Anders could indulge her, Binh shouted from a nearby table. He had a clipboard in his hand which he waved back and forth.

"What do you got there?" Anders asked, as he and Riese went to investigate. Anders snatched the clipboard and started reading. "Looks like an evacuation order. Signed by Director Phillipe Lacroix."

Binh pointed emphatically at the second paragraph.

"'Be sure to follow strict protocol,'" Anders read out loud. "'Infected test subjects must be euthanized, their bodies sealed and flown to designated dumping grounds. All other deceased should be loaded into pits on site for incineration.'"

"Euthanized," Riese said, gripping the back of her neck. "I thought this was a health clinic."

"In the middle of the jungle," Anders said. "Looks more like they were using people as guinea pigs and for some reason decided to cut and run, leaving a big mess behind."

Troubled shouts rang out. Anders pulled his inhibitor and rushed outside. Were they under attack? Khazanov and the others were nowhere in sight. Then came more shouting, this time from behind the clinic. They dashed in that direction. Turning the corner, Anders skidded to a stop, nearly falling into a massive pit piled high with charred corpses.

The others stood with pained expressions, staring down at the ghastly sight. Vacek made the sign of the cross and then covered his mouth and nose with his hand.

"I guess we just found those test subjects," Anders said, holstering his weapon.

Chapter 25

They were in the courtyard by the pergola now, Vacek looking like a guilty man about to come clean.

"This was a Genesis testing facility," he told them. "One of many built with the help of locals."

Khazanov let out a sardonic laugh. "By locals you mean they were using the Neanderthal natives as slave laborers," Khazanov said.

Vacek nodded. "That's one way of putting it. Their particular physiology made them a perfect choice for hard labor."

"Not that they had any say in the matter," Riese added.

Anders shook his head in disbelief. "That explains the ship we saw scooping them into that craft. So whose bodies are in that pit, Vacek? Whatever was left of your slave labor force after you were done with them? Or were they reassigned as test subjects?"

"Some were," Vacek said, choosing his words carefully. "Others were *Homo sapiens* subjects. The mandate was to create a vaccine, maybe even a cure. But apparently things got out of hand."

"You knew about this all along?" Riese said, outraged and still visibly in shock.

"Of course he did," Anders said, answering for him. "It's the real reason we're here, isn't it, Vacek?"

"Linking up with Gihon is still our primary objective, that hasn't changed."

Erwin's eyes grew wide. "So we can help a corporate entity that was conducting experiments on humans. You've got a lot of nerve."

"Don't you see what's at stake here?" Vacek shouted. "In the grand scheme of things it won't matter one bit how the cure was developed because without it the human race will surely go extinct."

"You had to have known we'd eventually discover the truth," Anders said. "But there's something else you're hiding. A high-tech facility like the one on that island doesn't just go offline for no apparent reason. And don't try to tell me they died off from infection. Something else happened and none of us are moving until you come clean."

Vacek's icy stare rose to meet Anders. "You wanna know why we're here? The real reason? Not that it'll change much, but I'll tell you. A week ago a dangerous psychopath named Phillipe Lacroix perpetrated a coup. He and his people killed the acting colonial director, took control of Gihon and then cut them off from the present."

"Why would they do that?" Riese asked.

"We believe he's holding the vaccine for ransom," Vacek said.

"So then what are your real orders?" Anders demanded. "And spare us any more bullshit."

Vacek smirked at the insult. "We're here to take back what's ours."

"Are you referring to the vaccine Genesis created by perpetrating one of the worst crimes against humanity since Adolf Hitler?" Erwin said.

"Beggars can't be choosers," Vacek replied with little emotion. "Would you prefer that billions of people die?"

"But why would Lacroix keep the vaccine for himself?" Riese asked. "Money?"

"Ideology," Vacek said. "Let's just say he's come to the conclusion that the world isn't worth saving."

Judging by the concerned looks on the faces of Vacek's men, it appeared that they'd also been kept in the dark on the finer details of the mission.

Erwin was pacing back and forth. "You've got to be kidding. Are you telling me you brought us here to be part of a hit squad?"

"Yes," Anders said. "But more than that, he's telling us our chances of going home are zero."

"We're expendable assets," Khazanov said. "Is that it?"

Vacek shook his head. "It may be hard to hear, but each and every one of us is expendable."

"Grieves mentioned we weren't the first group Genesis sent back," Anders said. "What happened to them, Vacek? Where are they?"

Vacek's eyes became glassy, warning Anders to stop while he was ahead.

"Dead, probably. There are a million dangers out here, if you haven't already noticed. Assuming, that is, they even made it here in one piece. Once Lacroix severed the portal on Gihon, the dangers of travelling to this time frame became infinitely greater."

"Then maybe we should set off on our own," Anders suggested.

Vacek and the other mercs burst into laughter. "You pussies wouldn't last two seconds out there. Hell, you couldn't find Gihon if it came up and bit you on the ass."

"Don't be so sure about that," Riese fired back, coming to the defense of Anders and the other scientists.

"I'm sorry to bruise your delicate egos," Vacek said, spittle forming at the corners of his mouth. "But in case you've missed the point so far, this mission is bigger than all of us. And we can't afford anything that's going to hold us back." Vacek's soulless gaze fell on Khazanov and his wounded leg.

The implication of Vacek's words was perfectly clear and Khazanov suddenly looked very worried. "I'm not the sort of man to beg," the Russian said. "But please don't leave me behind."

"No one's being left behind," Anders assured him. "We got into this together, we'll make it out together."

"You asked me what my orders were," Vacek said. "And I told you. Take back the colony at any cost and that's precisely what I intend to do." He removed his inhibitor, swiveled it and fired point blank at Khazanov's temple.

The Russian lurched over, his body convulsing. Anders cried out and tackled Vacek to the ground, the weapon flying from his hand. The two flailed around, punching and gouging.

Menacingly, the other three mercenaries turned to face Binh, Riese and Erwin.

Squaring his shoulders, the paleobotanist charged at Castleman, who absorbed the blow, even seemed to enjoy it. Erwin swung wildly as the brawny black merc blocked every strike with ease. He was toying with the scientist, enjoying every minute of it.

Stills moved in on Riese, a sick grin on his lips as he produced a ten-inch blade.

"You don't have to do this," she said, backing away.

131

"I've been dreaming about it since the first day we met."

"Then you may have to wait your turn," she said, motioning over his shoulder.

Stills glanced back and that was when Riese kicked him right between the legs. The merc grunted from the impact and then hissed out a long ragged breath. His face turned purple and he collapsed to the ground.

Seeing his comrade moaning in pain, Castleman flung Erwin aside and went for Riese. He didn't get more than a step before Binh hit him in the chest with a shot from Vacek's neural inhibitor. Down went Castleman, convulsing, his arms and legs pitched at odd angles like something out of a Picasso painting.

Halloway was the last man standing. He took a step toward Riese. Binh aimed the inhibitor at him and spoke in Boatese.

Halloway stopped. "What'd he say?"

"No idea," Riese said. "But if I had to guess I'd say it was something along the lines of, 'You feeling lucky, punk?'"

The medic raised his hands in surrender.

"Watch these three," she told Binh. "And if any of them move, light 'em up."

Binh flashed a gap-toothed smile.

On the floor Vacek and Anders continued to slug it out, although the soldier was quickly getting the better of him. Vacek had him in a full mount and was about to start raining down punches. Riese found a thick length of two-by-four which had fallen off the pergola and whacked Vacek over the head from behind. Momentarily stunned, he began to turn around when Riese gave him another taste, knocking him out cold.

Erwin helped Anders to his feet while Riese scooped up Stills' combat knife and slid it through her belt.

Anders stood on rubbery legs and rubbed his sore jaw. "You got one hell of a swing on you."

"I used to play t-ball," Riese said, almost embarrassed.

"Don't do nothing stupid," Halloway said in a pleading voice. "I wasn't gonna hurt no one, I swear."

"Here's what you can do," Anders told him, spitting out blood. "Check on Khazanov and hope to God he's okay."

Halloway scrambled over to Khazanov's prone form and set his fingers under his chin, feeling for a pulse. A moment passed, then two, before he looked up, fearful.

"Nothing."

Anders grabbed the inhibitor from Binh and aimed it at Halloway.

"Wait," Riese shouted. "You can't just shoot an unarmed man."

"Really?" he replied, a distinct lack of emotion. "Watch me."

He fired at Halloway, hitting him in the chest. The medic crumpled to the ground, his limbs quivering wildly.

"Don't worry," Anders reassured her. "When he finally wakes up, he'll feel like he downed a bottle of tequila. You heard Vacek before. A place like this is packed with dangers. Why should we be the ones to do the dirty work?" He turned to Erwin. "Go with Binh and find something we can tie them up with. I saw restraints on a few of the hospital beds we might be able to jury-rig. This world you dropped us into is an unforgiving place. Sooner or later something will come along to finish them off."

133

Chapter 26

An hour later, Anders, Erwin, Binh and Riese finally left
the biofacility. Even as they stepped back into the jungle,
Anders couldn't shake what Vacek had said before all
hell had broken loose.

You pussies wouldn't last two seconds out there.

Anders stopped the group, listening to the sounds of
the rainforest, breathing in greedy gulps of air heavy with
moisture. They'd taken the few remaining MRE's,
clothing and weapons—the last inhibitor and two combat
knives among them. But instead of wasting time taking
inventory then and there, they'd decided to take all of the
packs and sort through the contents later.

If they were careful, what remained might last a few
more days.

Anders checked his watch, as though he expected it
to somehow show him the way. The compass built into
the display indicated they were heading north. During
the initial briefing, it had been made clear they were
looking for an island situated off the coast of modern-

day Portugal—mind you, a country that wouldn't exist for another twelve thousand years.

Sea levels during the current period were much lower since millions of tons of water were still locked up in the ice sheets. As the climate began to warm over the next few thousand years, the glaciers would recede and raise seas levels by nearly two hundred feet. Which explained why the artifacts he'd discovered on the *Lady Luck* had been underwater.

But even that didn't explain the state of the archaeological site they'd come upon. Side scan sonar as well as visual contact from rovers had made it perfectly clear some kind of natural disaster had befallen the area—a massive volcanic eruption or perhaps an earthquake. Whether from rising tides or a natural disaster, the island they were searching for would eventually end up deep underwater.

He glanced over at Riese, who rested a hand against a tree while she drank from the water filtration bottle.

"I still can't stop thinking about poor Khazanov," Anders said, the anger boiling up inside him again.

"I miss his barreling laughter," Erwin said, with more than a touch of melancholy in his voice.

"The moment that spear punctured his leg," Riese said after taking another sip and wiping her mouth, "I had the sinking feeling he was a goner."

"The joys of studying microbiology," Anders said, forging ahead.

"Certainly makes it hard to look at the world," she replied. "Did you know there are more bacteria in your lower intestine than planets in the Milky Way galaxy?"

Anders shook his head, imagining how Khazanov with his weak stomach might have begged her to stop. "Given what lies ahead," he said, "I can't help but wonder whether he isn't the lucky one."

"There you go again," Riese said. "Throwing in the towel."

Anders furrowed his brow. "I don't know where you got that from, but I can assure you I finish everything I set my mind to."

"If you say so."

"Well, I'd love to know where you're getting your information from."

Riese tossed her hands in the air. "Hey, it's just the word on the street."

Erwin quickened his pace to catch up, ready to enjoy the show.

"So you spend your time listening to gossip, Dr. Riese? Is that what you're telling me?"

"You might call it gossip, but I call it speaking to people in the know. Listen, you had a falling out with your mentor and went your own way. Right or wrong, don't try to deny that Hiddenger's heart was shattered when you walked away."

"It wasn't personal," Anders said, his voice rising in frustration. "We had a professional difference of opinion. He wanted to keep searching for Atlantis around Santorini and I decided to take Plato at his word and head for the Atlantic. Did you know Hiddenger had been slated to join the team before he died?"

She nodded. "Khazanov told me."

"That seems a little strange, don't you think?"

"What are you saying? That Genesis is involved in some sort of conspiracy?"

"I'm not sure," Anders said. "Perhaps it's someone else who doesn't want them to succeed."

Riese seemed to consider this.

The group came to rest by a fallen palm tree. Binh dropped into a squat that Anders could never dream of duplicating.

"I don't know how you do that," Anders said.

Binh grinned, and brought his first two fingers to his lips.

"Of course I don't have a cigarette. Maybe if you'd ransacked Khan's office another few seconds, you might have found a carton or two."

"Did I miss something?" Riese asked, puzzled.

"If we ever make it out of this," Anders told Binh, "your wife is gonna find you and drag you home by the ear." Then to Riese. "You accused me of cutting and running, but I'll bet you didn't know that Binh here's the poster boy for skipping out on his responsibilities. How many kids do you have, Binh?"

Binh held up five fingers, then lowered all four except the middle one.

Anders smiled. "And what about you, Riese? What's your cross to bear?"

She pointed at Binh, who was still flipping the bird. "What he said."

Chapter 27

46 hours remaining

The rain started early the next morning and gave no sign of letting up anytime soon. Anders listened as the drops drummed against leaves and puddles collecting on the ground. They'd taken shelter beneath an outcropping of rock that had helped shield them from the worst of the inclement weather, although there was no real escape from the dampness. The fantasy of a hot shower and a full meal felt at once tantalizingly close and infuriatingly far. Taking a quick glance around, he saw that the other three were still sleeping, or what passed for sleeping under the current conditions. Most of the day would be spent trekking through more dense wilderness, an environment that had the depressing quality of all looking alike.

With pangs of hunger gnawing at his belly, Anders grabbed his pack and rooted through it for anything to eat. He finished the search a short time later, feeling disappointed and even hungrier. After he was done with his own pack, he began rooting through the heavy one they'd taken from Vacek. With reserved enthusiasm, Anders shuffled the contents around, hoping to hit pay dirt.

It wasn't long before he discovered that most of the space in Vacek's bag was filled by a small steel briefcase. He slid the heavy case out, setting it on the ground next to him.

But fancy equipment wasn't what he was searching for. With his penlight clamped between his teeth, Anders dove back into the pack, lifting the lip of the bag to gain a better look. Shoving his hand near the bottom, he caught the sound of a wrapper and the result was an almost instantaneous burst of joy. It seemed Vacek might have eaten his MREs, but he'd kept a stash of protein bars, peanut butter and chocolate, in reserve. Anders laid each one out on the metal case next to him, lining them up like little soldiers. There were eight in all. At the very least that meant two for each of them, assuming the other mercenaries' packs proved devoid of food.

Anders returned to the bars lined up on the metal case. Protein bars tasted like sawdust, but out here, in the rain and the heat, they were a godsend.

And Anders' good fortune didn't end there. He found two additional items at the bottom of the pack.

The first was a poncho. If ever there was a time this would come in handy it was now. The second discovery took him by surprise. It was a paperback book.

"Vacek, you grumpy bastard," Anders mumbled to himself. "I didn't take you for the reading type."

Nowadays, much like the watch on his wrist, physical books were largely the domain of antique dealers. But this one looked well-loved and frequently re-read.

139

Anders scanned the title, *The Life and Teachings of Epicurus*, and grunted. Apparently Vacek was a thinking man's brute. Philosopher and cold-blooded killer wrapped into one nasty package.

All in all, the choice of reading material seemed a strange one though, especially for Vacek. Epicurus, the fourth-century ancient Greek philosopher, had taught his followers to seek out a simple life, surrounded by friends and loved ones. A far cry from Vacek's current gig as a hired gun with a penchant for shooting innocent civilians in the head. A flash of Khazanov's final moments fought into his awareness. It left Anders with the blinding hope that something with long sharpened teeth might have already found Vacek and made a meal out of him.

Anders flipped through the pages and a small bookmark tumbled out. Scooping it up, he saw it was blank, but on the page it held, something was written in the margin.

Three numbers: 888.

Was it a date? August 8, 2048? The birthday of a child Vacek had hoped to return to, perhaps? Somehow, the thought left Anders upset. He preferred to think of the man who had killed his friend as little more than a psychopath. Why had he needed to cloud the situation by going through his things and risking seeing the man in a new light?

Anders snatched the protein bars, set seven of them back in the bag and tore the end from the eighth. His mouth watered as he took his first bite. Never mind that it was largely flavorless or took the jaw power of a grizzly to grind it down to size. He made a conscious decision to savor this moment and that was exactly what Anders did, listening to the rain drumming around him.

He was thoroughly one with his surroundings until, that was, his eyes settled back on the case. It did seem to be a strange item for even a soldier of fortune to bring with him, not to mention the paperback book. Vacek had forgone much of the standard equipment someone in his line of work would have brought with him. Was it the act of a man who hadn't thought he was going to make it back?

Anders lifted the case and set it in his lap.

Anders' father had owned a vintage Colt revolver from the eighteen sixties. He'd said it had once belonged to a Union officer who'd fallen at Gettysburg. The pistol was the old man's prized possession, one he'd kept locked away in a case much like the one in Anders' lap. Except while his father's case was mostly filled with high-density foam pistol inserts, this one was noticeably heavier.

The rain grew stronger, hammering the world outside their tiny shelter. The others around him were still asleep. Only Binh stirred, woken by the pounding rain.

Anders turned back to the briefcase. He tried to unlatch it only to discover the case was locked. Beneath the handle sat a three-digit rotary lock. The numbers were currently set to 463 on the left wheel and 379 on the right. He thumbed the tabs at either end, but they wouldn't budge. On a whim, he flicked both of them to read 888 and tried again.

Still nothing.

His frustration mounting, Anders was beginning to suspect the real locking mechanism was some sort of fancy biometric doohickey.

Instead of searching the case any further, he grabbed a nearby rock and used it to smash each of the latches. One by one they popped open. Anders sat in wonder, unable to keep from laughing. All that fancy technology brought down by a guy with a rock.

Carefully, he pushed open the lid and stared at the contents inside, trying to make sense of what he was

141

seeing. Silver cylinders crisscrossed with wires. Wedged between them was a timer. If Anders' heart hadn't leapt into his throat with the realization that he was holding a bomb, then it certainly did when he spotted the three-pronged symbol and the yield size on the underside of the lid.

But this wasn't just a bomb, was it?

It was a ten-kiloton suitcase nuke, powerful enough to annihilate everything within a one-and-a-half-mile radius.

He snapped it shut and pushed it off his lap.

Binh jerked awake then, asking why all the blood had drained away from Anders' face.

For a moment, Anders wasn't sure what to say. What good would it do? The real dilemma was figuring out what to do with it. Should they bury it in the ground or take it with them for someone on the island to dispose of? On the heels of that thought came something else. If this was a simple vaccine retrieval mission, then what was Vacek doing with a nuke?

"What's wrong?" Riese asked, propped up on one elbow. Over the last twenty-four hours they'd been beat up in every imaginable way and yet she still somehow managed to look good. Part of him wanted to let her know, but he wasn't yet certain how she'd take it.

Erwin was next to awaken and stretched his arms over his head in a frightening yawn.

"Where'd you get the briefcase?" Riese asked, sitting up straight. Her powers of observation were infuriating sometimes.

"Found it in Vacek's pack," he replied, trying to ignore her probing stare.

"Seems odd to carry a suitcase in a pack," Erwin said, scratching his head in confusion.

"That's what I thought. Until I opened it."

142

Riese's beautiful features grew tight. "What was inside?"

Anders held the case up to face them and lifted the lid.

They gasped.

"The hell?" Erwin screeched. "That looks like a bomb."

Binh's hands flew up in a dramatic flair, mimicking an explosion.

"Perhaps the mother of all bombs," Anders replied.

Riese shot to her feet, as though she were preparing to make a run for it. "Why would Vacek be carrying a nuclear device?"

"I'm not sure," Anders said. "Maybe he was ordered to destroy the colony."

"That doesn't make any sense," Erwin said, standing unevenly, his hands on his knees. "Why would Genesis go to all that trouble and expense of sending people back only to blow up the jewel in their crown?"

"They must really want this Lacroix guy dead," Riese said, rubbing her hands to keep warm.

Anders closed the case and set it aside, watching as the others followed it with their eyes. "Don't worry, it isn't armed," he told them. "I could drop it off a mountain and it wouldn't detonate."

Riese smirked. "I'll take your word for it."

Binh asked a question and Anders nodded in his direction. "I was wondering that myself. What exactly should we do?"

Riese cupped her hands, squeezing them nervously. "As I see it, we have two options. Bury it where no one will find it or take it with us."

"Take it with us?" Erwin exclaimed. "Are you mad? What if it goes off?"

"If it does," Anders said, "we'll be vaporized before our nerve endings have a chance to transmit the pain signals to our brains."

Riese let out a nervous laugh. "How reassuring." She paused to flick a drop of water from her forehead. "There's also Lacroix to consider. Grieves said he'd overthrown the previous leader in an ideological coup. Do we really want the power to destroy an entire city falling into the hands of a man who sounds more like a Third World dictator?"

Anders glanced down at his watch, remembering how they'd fished one just like it out of the Atlantic after Davenport had showed up with his shiny offer.

"There's one other thing no one's mentioned yet," Erwin said. "Don't forget those pills they made us swallow during the briefing."

"The nanites," Anders said, alarmed. "They may be tracking us already."

"And if we keep the suitcase," Riese said, following the argument to its logical conclusion, "then we would effectively be leading Vacek or members of a future expedition right to it."

With that the decision seemed obvious. They would bury the bomb in a place no one would ever find.

Chapter 28

Without wasting another moment, the group packed up their belongings and set off to find a place to bury the suitcase. From Anders' point of view, one location seemed about as good as another. The difficulty would be digging deep enough into the ground. For that they would use the combat knives they'd taken from the mercenaries to soften up a patch of wet earth and then scoop the contents out with their hands.

They selected an area far enough away from any large trees to avoid encountering a patch of thick roots. Binh and Anders were the first to start. They hacked and scraped at the jungle floor while being pelted from above by the incessant rainfall. Searching through their respective packs, the others had also found ponchos, for which they were very grateful. In the ruckus over the bomb, Anders had failed to mention their distinct lack of food.

After only minutes of tearing at the soil, Anders was out of breath. The work was backbreaking. Soon, Riese and Erwin took over, scooping out large handfuls of mud and torn-up roots and pushing them aside. After swapping places a few more times, the hole was deep enough for Anders to fit the case in before covering it over.

In years to come, as Mother Nature ate away at the case, the radioactive material would eventually spill out to contaminate this area, but there was nothing they could do about that. Sometimes you had to choose the least crappy option.

Finally finished, they stood by the buried case, staring down at their handiwork. The rain had let up some, becoming a misty haze as it trickled down through the canopy. The first sounds of the jungle after a storm were audible. Exotic birds cooing. Insects buzzing. The snap of a nearby branch. But something about that last sound triggered an almost prehistoric anxiety deep within Anders' belly. A noise which had come from behind them.

Anders spun. "You hear that?" he asked Binh, who listened and then shook his head.

"Must be a mouse, scurrying through the foliage," he told himself.

The sound came again, this time louder.

He unholstered the inhibitor and peered down at the status readout on the weapon's side. It was yellow and reading caution, which was another way of saying that the rain was playing havoc with the circuits inside.

Piece of crap!

Erwin started to march off. "Are you coming?"

More movement from the rear, this time lots of it as the culprit charged at them through the thick foliage. For a split second, Anders stood transfixed by the animal's rippling muscles, its powerful gait and above all the two large fangs protruding from its upper jaw. In a flash, he understood what they were facing: a sabertooth cat.

146

Perhaps the very one Vacek himself had said was tracking them near the biofacility.

Anders waved his arms frantically, shouting for his friends to run. There was something about abject terror that made the weight of the two packs he was carrying melt right away. Ahead of him, Riese and Binh broke into a sprint. Ten feet further still was Erwin, his legs pumping like an Olympic runner's. Anders bounded over a fallen tree, noticing they were on high ground. Which meant that they were less likely to get cornered by a cliff face or trapped in a canyon.

Breath rattling in his chest, Anders didn't dare look back, even though he could hear it slicing through the jungle, gaining on them with each stride. The beast's first move would be to bring him down with its claws. Once he was on the ground, it would follow up with a killing blow to the back of his neck. The mental image proved all the motivation Anders needed to keep moving as quickly as he could, his feet splashing through a small river of water three inches deep. He and the water on the ground were rushing in the same direction.

Then came the unsettling realization that he was alone. Riese, Binh and Erwin were nowhere in sight except for the fading sound of their cries.

Suddenly, the ground gave way and he was swept down in a mudslide. Outstretched branches and leaves scratched his face as he slid for what felt like forever. Soon he was dumped into a churning brown pond. Under he went, his nose filling with a mixture of sediment and water, bursts of pain shooting through his sinuses.

He came up gasping for air, rubbing at his eyes, searching to find the others. Not far away, a lifeless figure floated face down in the water and Anders rushed over. Upon reaching them, he pulled their head up and saw that it was Binh.

147

Chapter 29

"Hang on, little buddy," he told his friend, struggling against the muddy bottom as he made his way toward the water's edge. In his dread, thoughts of the sabertooth cat no longer registered. He had to get oxygen into Binh's lungs or Binh would die.

Once on land, Anders set Binh on his side to let the water drain from his lungs, but none came out. He checked and saw that his friend was breathing. At least that was good. A knot on Binh's forehead made it clear he'd collided with a rock or an overhanging branch on the way down.

With growing panic, Anders scanned his surroundings before spotting Riese dragging herself onto high ground along the opposite bank. He whistled to get her attention and then waved her over. By the time she arrived, cranky from having to wade back through the grimy pond, Binh was sitting up, coughing and sputtering.

"Have you seen Erwin?" he asked her.

Riese shook her head. "He was ahead of me. The next thing I knew my feet were up in the air and I was falling at a million miles an hour."

Anders couldn't help but grin. "Fun, wasn't it?"

"Not sure if that's the word I'd use, but I'll bet there's a lunatic or two back home who'd pay good money to take that ride." She cupped her hand over her eyes and searched the hillside. Multiple streams of muddy water flowed down from the top.

"Think he's still up there stuck on a branch or something?" she asked.

"Who knows?" Anders asked Binh what he remembered seeing.

The slight Vietnamese man merely shook his head. He wasn't all there yet.

"We can't stand around playing the guessing game," Anders decided. "And we're not gonna scale that hill. Let's just hope he got out somewhere else." He couldn't help thinking how that giant cat had followed them from the biofacility and might be lurking nearby.

"But he might be hurt somewhere," Riese protested.

Anders scanned the sky. "I don't think it's smart for us to go off searching with a sabertooth cat on our tail."

She agreed.

"Where's the other pack you were carrying?" he asked her. When they'd stripped the mercenaries of their equipment, Riese had taken Castleman's pack, along with her own. Now she only had Castleman's.

Riese looked around in dismay, her face caked with patches of mud. "Musta come off." She slapped her leg and cursed. "I was using Castleman's as my main because it was heavier and now I've lost all my clothes."

At least she still had something. When Anders had fished Binh out of the water, Binh hadn't been wearing a pack at all.

The stark implication was that they were down to the seven power bars in Anders' pack along with his inhibitor and one water filtration bottle.

Riese removed Castleman's pack and set it down so they could quickly go through it. The top layer was mostly wet clothing. Socks, briefs, a purple Speedo bathing suit. Binh made a comment and Anders couldn't help but laugh.

"What'd he say?" Riese inquired, not wanting to be left out.

"He asked if Castleman thought he'd be hitting a beach." Anders removed the items and tossed them aside. "Wet clothes are only going to slow us down." Underneath they found a tablet in a watertight case. He removed it and powered it on. The screen flickered to life, briefly showing the Genesis logo. Slowly a map came into view.

"Any idea where we are?" Riese asked, peering over his shoulder.

Anders shook his head. "Judging by this, I'd say smack dab in the middle of nowhere."

Binh reached over and tapped the screen with his finger, changing the view. A series of dots appeared on the display.

"Hey," Anders said. "How'd you do that?" He glanced down at the new overlain image. In the center were three blinking blue dots. "This must be us," he reasoned. After he pinched the image to shrink it down, the coastline suddenly came into view. A legend at the bottom gave an approximate distance.

"Looks like we're twenty miles from the Mediterranean," Anders said.

A blinking yellow dot drew his attention.

"That's strange." He zoomed in and saw that the yellow icon was less than a mile away and it seemed to be moving, albeit slowly. His gaze met Riese's. "Could it be Erwin?" he wondered.

"I suppose," Riese said, not sounding convinced. "Perhaps if he were somehow swept down the hill in a different direction and went searching for us." She stopped, her hand frozen in the act of rubbing mud off her face. Tiny droplets of mist-like rain had collected in her hair. "Could it be someone else?"

"You mean one of the mercs?"

"I'm not sure. It's possible."

"They weren't dumb enough to swallow those pills," Anders said. "Remember?"

"Why the different color?" she asked, thin threads of fear settling into her voice. "If it was Erwin, wouldn't he be blue?"

"There's only one way to find out." Anders tossed Castleman's pack to Riese and helped Binh to his feet.

Riese sighed, her piercing blue eyes practically pleading with Anders. "I was afraid you'd say that."

They set off, wet and miserable and hoping that every painful step might bring them closer to home.

Chapter 30

Erwin came awake to the sound of rushing water. A quick, groggy look around revealed he was draped over the base of a tree that had sprouted up from the hill at a forty-five-degree angle. His head hurt something awful. Slowly the memories of what had happened came flooding back, no pun intended.

Something had been chasing them through the jungle when the ground beneath his feet had opened up and swallowed him. He remembered speeding down a river of brackish water only to ping-pong off an outstretched branch and onto the tree upon which he presently found himself. Thirty feet below him, the runoff from the mountain rain collected in a small body of murky water.

Ignoring the throbbing pain in his head, Erwin pushed himself from his perch and began scaling down the hill, careful to stay away from the powerful currents of mud surging on either side of him.

Once on solid ground, he scanned the area for the other members of his party.

That feeling of panic brewing in his chest since he'd opened his eyes and started down the hill now ratcheted up a notch.

Was the beast that had sprung out at them still on the loose?

"Stay calm, Doctor," he told himself, as he always did when his emotions began running high. "Keep your wits about you and we'll find a way out of this."

With a backpack empty of food and the weapon from his holster now long gone, Erwin kept replaying Vacek's taunt.

You pussies wouldn't last two seconds out there.

He cupped his hands around his mouth, called out each of their names and listened as nothing but his own voice echoed back at him. Perhaps they had drowned somewhere in this murky bog, their bodies already in the process of decomposing, their bellies filling with gases which would eventually force them to the surface. A gruesome thought, but Erwin quickly realized it was more likely they had splashed into the pond, seen he wasn't anywhere in sight and left without giving it another thought.

And why was he not surprised? He was a graduate from Princeton with a degree in paleobotany, perhaps the youngest director of the Peabody museum ever, a man with well over three hundred academic papers to his name. No doubt about it, Erwin had his fair share of accolades. But what he'd lacked his entire life was the sort of dynamic personality that not only drew people to him, but kept them around. The sort of disposition that would have prompted them to perform at least a cursory search before leaving him for dead.

Working his way back into the thicket, Erwin nearly tripped over a branch lying across his path. He cursed and picked it up to give it a good toss when he noticed the sharpened edge. The body was about an inch thick and it was shaped like a spear. For a man in the wild with nothing to protect him, what at first had seemed like an annoyance now made him feel like the king of the jungle. A vine or two to swing on while he beat on his chest was all he needed.

Erwin had no sooner finished relishing the mental image when the rustling of leaves drew his attention. He dropped down low, hoping to high hell it wasn't the thing that had chased them through the rainforest. For a moment, he shut out the sounds of birds and insects in the distance, even the grumbling of his own belly, empty since this morning when he'd taken a single bite of Anders' power bar. Now, with nothing to eat, he was beginning to wonder if he was next on the menu for whatever was rattling that bush.

Erwin held his breath as the creature emerged and the sight of it nearly made him wet his pants with relief. The galagos stepped into a small clearing and regarded him. A small primate with a long bushy tail and an equally large set of eyes, it looked more like an overgrown squirrel than it did a relative of the monkey. They were mostly seen at night, which lent the sighting an even greater significance.

Erwin found himself standing with the spear in his outstretched arm. He was getting ready to throw it, an unconscious impulse driven by the hunger in his belly.

"And then what, you doofus?" he chided himself. He didn't know the first thing about butchering an animal. Hell, he'd been a teenager, growing up in Queens, when he'd first realized that food didn't spring into existence on grocery store shelves.

Not far from the galagos he spotted a *Nepenthes attenboroughii*, or what some called a rat-eating pitcher plant. He approached and bent down next to it. Named after the famous naturalist and documentary filmmaker David Attenborough, it was said to be the largest

154

carnivorous plant on earth, capable of consuming all manner of rodents in the acidic enzymes it stored in its vessel-like belly.

Other, equally wonderful species, many presently extinct, stood nearby and Erwin had to fight the urge to drop down to study each and every one of them. At least Khan had been right about one thing. Stepping away from the textbooks and observing the past first-hand was a one-of-a-kind experience.

Then Erwin made a discovery that would change everything. Maybe ten feet away he spotted a patch of wild horned cucumbers. Built much like a regular cucumber, this particular species was yellow and covered in thorny spikes. They weren't the prettiest of vegetable, but that only meant everyone in the expedition would have walked right by them. Which highlighted another benefit of Erwin's academic background. He recognized they were edible. A cursory glance at the brush around him also revealed at least two other leaves he could eat.

In his panic he hadn't been thinking clearly. He didn't need to run himself ragged, trying to spear, skin and then cook animals. Not when the jungle provided more than enough sustenance just waiting to be plucked from the ground. Maybe food didn't just pop into existence on grocery store shelves, but he couldn't help thinking that this was the next best thing.

Chapter 31

Prague, Czech Republic August 15, 2059

The monk was seated at a quaint street side café on the corner of Kaprava and Zatecka, sipping an espresso and listening to police sirens howling down the city's narrow cobbled streets. Nearby, a group of young partygoers passed by, whispering in the muted way Czech people tended to. They couldn't possibly know, but Dr. Gustave Hiddenger was dead. More than that, he'd been blown to bits, his remains scattered over a stretch of Celetna Street. In an hour it would be all over the online news service. And yet with only a dozen blocks between him and the crime scene, the monk was safe. It would take the police hours and maybe even days before they caught the faintest glimmer that the man had been assassinated.

The monk pulled the disposable phone from his pocket and dialed a number.

"Yes." The voice on the other end sounded tired. Father Yohann had been sleeping.

"It's done," the monk said, tilting back what was left of his espresso, then carefully setting the cup on the table.

Silence on the other end. "And the others on the list?"

"Hiddenger was the last."

"Well done," Yohann said, pleased. His mentor was normally thrifty with praise and the delight in his voice was unmistakable. "There is something else I need you to do. A set of instructions awaits you on the Charles Bridge, at the feet of Saint Wenceslas. Report back when you've read them."

The line went dead.

The monk fished a few Czech crowns from his pocket, set them under the cup and headed to collect the new orders Father Yohann had mentioned.

Approaching the Charles Bridge, he could see lights from the picturesque Prague castle twinkling off the Vltava River. The statue Father Yohann had directed him to actually featured three saints, not one. The monk set a foot on the railing and raised himself up. As promised, a slip of folded paper sat wedged in a narrow space beneath Wenceslas' robe. The monk unfolded the note and read what was written.

A package awaits you under the bed of your hotel room. After you retrieve it, a private plane will bring you back immediately. Once you see the package, you'll understand.

The monk removed the lighter from his pocket, set fire to the paper and let the breeze pull it from his fingers and down toward the river.

With every step back to the hotel, the monk's heart beat more ferociously in his chest. But not because of the sound of sirens, growing all the more distant. The

157

culmination of his mission was fast approaching and he was eager to fulfill his destiny.

When he arrived, the clerk at the reception desk nodded as he entered. Overhead, the TV was showing some breaking news.

"Have you heard?" the night clerk asked in broken English. The light overhead made the oily skin on his young face glisten.

The monk paused in the act of calling the elevator. "About the explosion?"

The clerk looked confused. "What explosion?"

The monk furrowed his brow. "Never mind." He took a deep breath, admonishing himself for speaking out of turn. "What happened?"

"That frozen body they found in Spain," he said, a mix of fear and excitement crowding his voice. "It's released a deadly virus."

Nodding, the monk punched the elevator button.

"They said the local government was trying to keep it hushed up, but things spiraled out of control."

The doors opened and the monk stepped inside. "You can't trust anyone these days, can you?" the monk said.

The clerk agreed as the doors closed on his worried face.

In his hotel room, the monk found a silver suitcase under his bed, just as the note had promised. The code beneath the handle read 888. Sacred numbers for the Epsilon Brotherhood. Placed on its side, the number eight was also the symbol for infinity. The three digits represented the three stages of wisdom: thesis, antithesis and synthesis. He plucked the dog-eared book he was reading off the table and scribbled the numbers into one of the margins.

Inside the case, the monk found the components for a suitcase-sized nuclear device, the sight of which immediately made the pores on his forehead open up with beads of perspiration. The second was a note he read while struggling against the growing tremor in his hands.

You've trained extensively with dummy bombs, the note read. *What lies before you is the real thing. Return to the* Excelsior *at once and resume the cover we've provided you. Deliver the device to Gihon and wipe it from the face of the earth. The survival of the world's faithful depends on your success. Godspeed.*

The monk shut the case and reset the security code. As he finished, he caught sight of the tattoo on the underside of his wrist: the five interlocking rings of the Epsilon Brotherhood. A tremendous responsibility had been placed on his shoulders and he prayed that when the time came he would be able to fulfill his duty.

•••

Now in the rain-soaked jungles of Neolithic North Africa, Vacek stood staring at the very same tattoo. In the short time since his mission to Prague had ended, everything that could go wrong had gone wrong. It was a perfect example of Murphy's Law in action. The still-painful sting that he and his men had been bested by a bunch of bookworms was hard to endure, but worse was the knowledge that they'd also stolen the suitcase nuke, the very heart of his mission for the Brotherhood. Vacek hadn't spent years climbing through the ranks at Genesis, cultivating his secret identity as a key player in the company's security force, only to fail at the most critical juncture. The truth was, he'd underestimated them. They all had, but it was a mistake he would never make again.

His gaze shifted to the restraints which now lay in a wet heap at their feet. Heavy rain washed over him, clearing the blood from the back of his head where Riese had struck him with that length of two-by-four. He raked his eyes skyward, letting his mouth fill with thick droplets of rain. His first order of business would be to find that case. Next would be to show those scientists what happened to those who crossed him.

"They've got at least a six-hour headstart on us," Stills said as he searched the nearby area for anything useful the scientists might have left behind. Even with the passage of a good few hours, Stills was walking like a man whose testicles had been caught in a vice. More than once he stopped to relieve the pain by shifting the seat of his black cargo pants.

The pronounced scowl on Castleman's face made it more than clear that he too was itching for revenge on whoever had lit him up with the inhibitor. He'd awoken on the ground long after the scientists were gone, twitching in a puddle of his own saliva. They'd even shot Halloway, who had woken up rubbing a singe mark on his chest rig.

"It won't matter how much of a headstart they have," Vacek told his men.

Halloway was behind him, disinfecting the wound at the back of his head. In one of the few pieces of good fortune, the scientists had left most of the medical supplies in their haste to flee.

"They have no training," Vacek went on. "If the large predators don't get them, then we will. Every moment that goes by, gentlemen, our job gets easier and easier."

Stills chuckled. "I hope you're wrong, because I got a bone to pick with Riese and I got a feeling she ain't gonna like me much when I'm done."

Castleman returned to the group and dropped four crude-looking spears on the ground. He then pulled up his pant leg to reveal a folding knife in a leather case tied beneath his right knee. Unlatching the blade, he began to sharpen the end of the first stick.

Halloway's eyes grew wide when he saw the blade. "Now you pull out a knife? That woulda been handy when I was working my fingers to the bone trying to untie those knots."

Castleman grunted without looking up from his whittling.

Vacek yanked back his sleeve, revealing the OLED display on his wrist. After powering it on, he waited for a map of the area to appear. Slowly, a series of colored dots populated the display screen. The three blue dots represented the scientists. Vacek had expected to find four, which implied that one of them might have been killed. Another dot was yellow and the three blues were heading toward it.

A faint signal showed up briefly before disappearing. It was a fourth blue dot more than a mile behind the others. Perhaps he was wrong about one of the scientists being dead. They were proving to be more durable than he expected.

Castleman handed him a sharpened spear. "Might not be a rifle with explosive rounds, but for our purposes it should do just fine."

Stills grabbed his and hefted it in the air. He'd scooped mud off the ground and streaked his face with it. "I always wanted to go native."

The others did the same and suddenly they looked less like a band of mercs and more like a tribe of headhunters.

Vacek turned to the others. "Grab what you can. We're moving out."

161

Chapter 32

Anders studied the steady yellow blip on the tablet as they weaved through a patch of bamboo trees. Next to him, Riese braced a hand against every tree they passed as she struggled along. Bringing up the rear was Binh, peering back along the ground they'd just covered every few seconds to ensure nothing was attempting to sneak up on them.

It had been more than an hour since they'd last seen Erwin. Already, Anders had started to convince himself that the yellow dot would lead them to the lost member of their group.

"You need a rest?" Anders asked Riese.

"I need a new pair of shoes," she said. "And a dry set of clothes. Since you're asking, might as well throw in a hot shower and a massage."

He laughed. "The massage I can manage, but I wouldn't hold your breath on the rest."

She smiled. Their eyes met. Embarrassed, she quickly looked away. "What do you figure our chances are of making it out of this?" she asked.

"Hard to say," he replied, navigating over an outcropping of rock. He turned to lend her a hand and she accepted. "I guess we'll only know if we make it to Gihon."

"Not if, when," she corrected him. "My mother always taught me to be positive."

Anders pursed his lips. "She sounds like a smart woman," he said.

She nodded, her eyebrows lifting ever so slightly. "In some ways, she was."

"I sense some hesitation."

"Well, not that it's any of your business, but we never really saw eye to eye. I suppose that's the polite way of putting it."

Anders stopped and offered her a pull from the water bottle. She obliged and passed it along to Binh, who drained what was left.

"That doesn't surprise me one bit," Anders said, taking the bottle back and storing it away. "Two women with strong personalities. You probably tore each other to shreds."

"You might say that," Riese admitted. "But you'll never guess why."

There was a challenge in her statement and Anders was more than happy to take the bait. He scratched the stubble on his chin and planted his hands on his hips as he considered the most likely possibility. "Your mother never really wanted kids and resented you for being born."

"Ouch," Riese said. "Harsh and imaginative, but you're way off. My mother didn't believe—even in today's day and age—that a woman should work, let alone as a scientist."

163

Anders was genuinely surprised. "Really? I thought she would have been proud of what you've accomplished."

"A PhD in molecular virology from Harvard Medical School followed by an assistant professorship in the Department of Microbiology and Immunobiology the following year, several published papers in the field, more than one of them groundbreaking in determining how RIG-I and MDA5 cytosolic receptors induce an antiviral type-I interferon response, and she still wasn't happy. Her faint praise was always followed by, 'You really should have gone into modeling. Traveled the world, rubbed shoulders with celebrities.'"

"So in her way of thinking, you just never measured up," Anders said. They were standing in a grove of majestic fifty-foot trees.

"Something like that," Riese replied. The pain on her face was apparent. "She believed a woman's singular asset was her beauty. The better I did in school, the worse our relationship became, until one day we had a blowout and haven't talked since."

Binh spoke and Anders nodded.

"Binh thinks your mom was jealous and I think he might be right."

"Jealous?" Riese repeated the word with incredulity.

"I worked my way through school tending bar in a seedy joint outside Cape Town," Anders said, "and believe me, I've heard everything under the sun. If I had a dollar for every time some poor schmuck complained how his father was trying to tear him down, I woulda been rich enough to tell Davenport where he could stick his offer."

Riese was scanning the jungle floor. "I guess I never thought about it that way," she said. "I mean, I'd always assumed she wanted the best for me."

Anders shook his head and laid a hand on Riese's shoulder. "Sounds to me like she was pissed off that her daughter had the whole package. Sharp as a whip with a face that could melt steel."

Riese looked up at him, blushing.

"And don't fool yourself about the human race, we're one messed-up species," he said, Binh next to him nodding vigorously. "You might not see it 'cause you got that pretty face of yours buried in microscopes all day. But do yourself a favor and study history for a change and you'll see how ugly we can be to one another."

Anders' gaze fell to the tablet in his hand and the breath hitched in his throat. The yellow dot was gone. A second later, he realized that wasn't right. It wasn't gone, it was hovering over the three blue ones.

Just then, a shape reached out from behind a nearby tree and pressed the cold steel of a blade against his throat. A single name fired through his startled mind.

Vacek.

Riese gasped and took an unsteady step back.

The six-inch knife was lashed to the tip of a bamboo spear. From the other end came the sound of a ragged voice. "Move a muscle and I'll split your neck from ear to ear."

Chapter 33

The man stepped out from behind the tree and circled around, the knife still trained on Anders' throat. He seemed in bad shape. Dark circles ringed his eyes and the flesh on his face was translucent, like he'd been hiding for days, or maybe even weeks. Apart from the bushy brown beard covering his face, there wasn't another hair on his head.

The man's tattered blue coverall was exactly like their own, except the stranger had cut the arms and legs off.

Binh pulled Riese behind him. The stranger's eyes grew wide. "Nobody move," he shouted. "Didn't you hear me?"

Anders stuck a hand up, palm out, signaling his two companions to stay put. "We heard you just fine, pal, now just take it easy," Anders said. "We have no beef with you."

"You expect me to believe that?" he fired back. "I see what you're wearing. You work for them. You've

166

come to kill me." Tears formed in the man's swollen eyes.

The fear had temporarily sapped his determination and Anders grabbed the spear with one hand and shoved the man back with the other. He went tumbling to the floor with all the resistance of a small child.

Anders tossed the spear to Binh and then stood over the crazed man, offering his hand. "If we'd really come here to kill you," he said, "you'd be dead by now." He wiggled his fingers and the man reached out, lifting himself off the ground.

"I was sure you were one of them," he said, brushing the dead leaves from his filthy clothes.

"One of who?" Riese asked. "Genesis?"

He shook his head. "I don't know. They captured two of our party and the rest..." His voice trailed off.

"Where are they?" Anders asked. "The people you came back with."

"Dead," he shouted. "They're all dead. And so will we be if we stay here."

"You have a camp?" Riese asked.

"I guess you could say that. I tried for a room at the Four Seasons, but they were all booked up."

Binh smiled, but neither Riese nor Anders were laughing. Whoever this guy was, he'd spent too much time on his own.

"Are you hungry?" Anders asked. "I've got food and we can filter some fresh water. It's not much, but it's all I have."

He agreed and they followed the man back to his camp. On the way, Anders saw that he was favoring his left ankle, trying not to put too much pressure on it. He wondered whether this was the wounded man Grieves had told them about.

Before long, they arrived at a small clearing. A rock large enough to sit on had been rolled next to a fire pit.

167

But apart from that, there was no tent or makeshift shelter. Scattered about were the bones of what looked like rats and small game.

The man went to a fallen tree, peeled back a piece of bark and reached a hand in. Fishing back and forth for a second, he produced a giant white larva. It squirmed in his grasp, trying to bite with its pincers. He looked at Riese. "Do you want yours cooked?"

Her skin turned the color of clean linen. "Thanks, but I had bugs for breakfast."

"Your loss," he said and shoved the thing into his mouth, bursting it between his teeth.

Anders reached out and grabbed a hold of Riese before she could faint.

Binh went over to the tree and snatched a larva for himself.

His Vietnamese friend was already on his second larva when Anders could no longer hide his disgust. "You're enjoying that, aren't you?" Anders asked.

Binh nodded enthusiastically and went for a third.

"You better not talk to me with that bug breath after."

Eager to shift this strange encounter in a different direction, Anders introduced each of them.

"Name's James Pritchard," the man told them, wiping his hands on his chest. "But you can call me Jim."

"How long you been here, Jim?" Anders asked.

Jim's eyes flickered toward the canopy. "Don't rightly know," he said. "A week, maybe more. Those Genesis morons dumped us in the middle of a lake. That was when we lost the first member of our party. Dragged ourselves to shore and things quickly went from bad to worse."

"Sounds like a bad case of déjà vu," Anders said.

Jim grinned. "You too, eh? Well, I figure we won't be the last. The corp's determined to take back what's

168

theirs and get that vaccine. I'm sure they'll send as many folks as it takes."

"They don't know their coordinates are off," Riese said.

"How could they?" Jim snapped. "No one's made it back yet. Not since Lacroix declared himself emperor."

"Emperor or not," Anders said, "we need to find a way home."

"To the future?" Jim asked, incredulous.

Riese gave him a puzzled look. "Of course. You make it sound like a bad thing."

"This world might not be much, but in case you haven't heard, the one back home is fast becoming a disease-infested garbage dump."

"Isn't that why we're here?" Anders reminded him. "To bring back the vaccine and change all that."

Jim let out a long raspy laugh. "What makes you think Lacroix will give it up?"

"Because without it, billions will die," Riese said.

Jim's eyebrows arched. "This one's a handful," he said, indicating Riese. "I can see it already."

Binh ignored the comment and asked a question.

"The hell did he say?" Jim barked. "I don't speak boat people."

"It's Boatese," Anders corrected him. "And he asked what your role was in the group you returned with."

"I'm a pilot. Made my living making runs out to container ships in the Mediterranean. Whenever some poor deckhand slob got sick and needed an evac, I got the call. Was approached by some strange bird named Davenport. Found me in a bar having a drink one night, offered a lot of money if I'd fly a Cutter on a 'simple rescue mission.' Whole thing sounded whacko at first, but hey, who could turn down that much dough, right? Was only after they sent us back here that I heard the guy I was supposed to replace had been found in a public bathroom with his throat slit. Guess I shoulda listened to my gut and told Davenport to cram it up his tailpipe."

"How do we get to Gihon?" Anders asked him, trying to cut through the static.

Jim only shook his head. "I know this ain't what you wanna hear, but you should stay away from those fascist bastards."

"How can we?" Riese protested. "It's our only way home."

"That may be so, but if you listen long enough, you'll hear one of their ships passing overhead. They're shuttling dead bodies into mass graves they got all over the place."

"We saw one of their… research labs," Anders said.

"Then you know they have no regard for life, human or otherwise. They been snatching primitive people the way Europeans snatched Africans hundreds of years ago. Some are forced into slavery, others become lab rats. I'm not sure which is worse."

Anders nodded, remembering the disturbing scene of the natives being rounded up like cattle. "Even so," Anders said, "we're not going to lie down and die in the jungle. Tell us how to get to Gihon."

"There's a port city along the coast called Xanbar," Jim told them.

"Xanbar," Anders repeated under his breath. "Sounds like a place with cold drinks and loose women." Binh cackled laughter while Riese crossed her arms, unimpressed.

"From there, you should be able to catch a ride to the island. At least, that was the plan before our group went to hell."

"What do you mean?" Riese asked, concerned.

"Didn't realize at the time, but one of the mercs accompanying us was a mole, working for the Epsilon

170

Brotherhood. Killed three members of our group before he was tackled. The team leader spent an hour working him over before the truth finally came out. Sorry bastard died on us before we could get any more out of him."

Anders thought at once of the suitcase bomb he'd found in Vacek's pack. "They want to destroy Gihon," he blurted out.

Binh and Riese stared at him.

"Damn right they do," Jim exclaimed. "Seems they're afraid someone on this side might tinker with history. Do something crazy that might stop Jesus or Buddha from ever being born."

Pieces were falling into place and the implication left them in stunned silence. In the background, the sounds of the jungle grew louder.

Jim turned to Anders, his face serious. "You were followed," he said.

Anders regarded him with a look of confusion. Was he somehow talking about Vacek? Or worse, the sabertooth?

Jim aimed his index finger at a clump of bamboo trees. "Not sure what you did, but you seem to have made a friend."

All three turned and scanned the spot Jim had pointed to. From out of his hiding place came the half-Neanderthal boy, Aku, carrying a small spear and eyeing each of them with the shit-eating grin of a boy who'd been up to no good.

Chapter 34

To many of his friends—and even his enemies—Dr. Daniel Erwin was about as close to being a genius as a man could come. By the age of nine he'd completed high school and by twelve had had his first university degree. At fifteen, his face still dotted with teenage acne, he'd received his PhD in paleobotany from Princeton University.

However, Erwin's real contribution to the field would come five years later when he revolutionized the study of fossil leaves. Always an obsessive organizer, Erwin had meticulously documented the vein patterns in plants and used the data to completely redraw a century-old classification model.

But for all of his formidable intellectual prowess, Erwin still had trouble with the simple things, like operating a washing machine, holding a conversation or figuring out the precise moment he'd blown his chances with a member of the opposite sex.

Erwin had become known to those around him for two main quirks. The first was his insistence his students remove their shoes before entering his classroom. The second was his terrible sense of direction.

The latter had meant that the three miles heading north he'd covered after losing Anders, Riese and Binh had actually been spent heading east. Also lost on him were the large swaths of rainforest he saw for the second and third time. What he did have was a pack comfortably filled with wild horned cucumbers, *Grewia* fruits and kram kram, an edible plant whose seeds, in modern times, were considered a famine food in areas such as Chad and the Sudan. In addition, he'd also stopped to collect over a dozen samples from plants now extinct in the twenty-first century, specimens he hoped to one day return to the wild.

Eager to link up with the other members of his party, Erwin pushed on. He was growing more confident by the hour that their meager food stocks would soon be running out. More than anything, he relished the idea of playing the savior. He took another bite from the horned cucumber in his hand and let the remnants fall to the ground. Perhaps then Riese might soften that thorny outer skin she used to shield herself from scrutiny.

In Erwin's other hand was his walking stick and spear. With his knowledge of the jungle's true abundance, there was no need for such things as conservation or frugality.

With a myriad of self-aggrandizing thoughts swirling through his head, Erwin failed to register the unusual silence in the rainforest. It was only when the earth began to tremble that he recognized something was amiss.

Pulse quickening, Erwin planted his feet and scanned his surroundings. Nothing seemed out of place, although in the dense jungle, it was common to never actually see what was coming at you.

As the noises grew louder, so too did trumpet blasts from elephants on the march. Without thinking, he headed toward the cacophony, soon finding himself at the sharp edge of a twenty-foot cliff.

Stretching for perhaps a mile beneath him was a lush valley. Down below to his left was a watering hole and an impossibly long line of elephants heading toward it. Erwin took a closer look. Unlike the typical African gray elephant, the ones before him were chestnut-colored with long curved tusks.

As fast as the charging animals came the realization that these weren't elephants at all. The creatures below were a cousin of the woolly mammoth, but larger and with far less fur. Such majestic beasts were mesmerizing to behold. Travelling in a group of fifty or more, they approached the water's edge. At a hundred yards' distance, they might have been too far to touch, but they weren't too far to get a picture of. He removed the camera in its watertight case from his pack, and crawled as close as he could to the edge in order to take a picture. In doing so, he curled his feet around the stalks of a pair of young saplings to brace himself. Even at only twenty feet up, there would be no way to scale the sheer cliff face if he tumbled over the edge. He also knew how quick to anger a herd of mammoths would be, especially when accompanied by their young.

After a half-dozen photos, Erwin was getting ready to take a mosaic of the entire valley when a pair of rough hands grabbed hold of his ankles. He shrieked as they thrust him forward, half his body hanging over the outcropping. His cries of terror must have startled the group of mammoths, because two males peeled off from the herd and began charging in his direction.

"Oh, for God's sake, pull me up," he begged. The hands held him firm. Whenever he tried to wiggle his body to see who it was, they lowered him another six inches. Rocks tumbled over the side as the mammoths closed the distance. Fifty feet, then forty, thirty and before he knew it they were right on top of him, preparing to impale him with their deadly tusks. Erwin closed his eyes and sobbed for mercy.

"I'll do anything, just don't let me die."

Sharp rocks tore at his stomach as he was yanked up. The powerful grip on his ankles let go and Erwin curled into a ball, slobbering.

"I don't like little boys who cry," the voice said and Erwin knew right away who it was.

Chapter 35

Aku knelt in the brush and signaled for Anders and Riese to do the same. He pinched his lips between his forefinger and thumb. A strange-looking sign, but Anders knew precisely what it meant. Keep quiet.

About fifty yards away an adolescent wild boar rooted through the dirt. As hunting targets went, it might not be quite as dangerous as its parent, but certainly nothing to laugh at.

The three of them were armed with flint-tipped spears. Finding the rock had been the easy part. Chipping the stone to a razor-sharp edge had been something else entirely. And this was where Anders' affinity for experimental archaeology had come into play. Even as a graduate student back in Cape Town, he'd shunned the discipline's obsessive reliance on book learning alone. Over the years, caves throughout Europe had been replete with sharpened flint speartips as well as the cutting and scraping tools essential to their ancestors' way of life. For many years, modern man's intimate understanding of how these things were made had been sorely lacking.

Flint knapping, as the process was called, involved striking a piece of flint with a hammerstone at an angle in order to whittle it into the desired shape. Pressure flaking was the next stage. The goal there was to refine the point. That was accomplished by pressing a thin piece of horn along the edge of the blade. After hours of trial and error in the university lab, he'd managed to knock out a decent-looking specimen.

Back in camp Aku had watched patiently as Anders had plied his skills. Afterward, the child had held it up to the light and tossed it aside, a move which had given Binh a bout of roaring laughter. The kid then took a fresh piece of flint and banged out one of superior quality in a fraction of the time, and all without needing any other tool than a small hammerstone. The sight was impressive and, watching it, Anders couldn't help but wish that Khazanov was here to see it too. The big Russian would have looked on with the delight of a child eyeing Santa's elves cobbling Christmas presents.

The smell of the fetid ground grew stronger as Anders and Riese lowered themselves behind a giant leaf. It was a unique mix of earth with a smoky musk found nowhere else.

Excitement aside, this little hunting excursion wasn't purely educational. Not long after the larvae buffet, Anders and Riese had finished the last of the protein bars, which meant that from here on in, they needed to either develop a love for eating insects or find an alternative source of protein.

Riese leaned in and whispered into his ear. "Have you wondered at all why he's been following us?" She was referring to Aku, but Anders was still relishing the feeling of her warm breath against his neck.

177

"Figured he was lost."

"Don't be thick," she admonished him, trying nevertheless to keep quiet. "He's an orphan."

Anders turned and saw she was serious. "An orphan? How on earth would you know that?"

She looked away for a moment. "He told Khazanov his mother was dead."

Anders sighed. "So then how is that our problem?"

"It's not," she said defensively. "I'm only pointing it out. You seem to be studying him as though he were a living exhibit and I wanted to remind you he's also a person."

"If anyone needs to be reminded of that it's Lacroix, not me."

The two scientists fell into an uncomfortable silence while they waited for Aku to send them a signal.

"Oh, this is ridiculous," Anders snapped.

"What's he doing?" Riese asked, a disproportionate amount of fear in her voice.

Anders could tell the horror of a failed hunt and the possibility of a mouthful of squirming larvae was starting to get to her.

"I thought the plan was to charge after the boar, but instead he's staring at something on the ground." The camp wasn't more than a mile away and Anders' mouth was already watering with the thought of freshly killed meat cooking over an open fire. Peering over the leaf, he watched the boar finish foraging and scurry off. Swearing, Anders rose and marched over to Aku, still kneeling in a clump of bushes.

"What exactly was the holdup?" he asked. "We just watched a perfectly good piece of meat scamper away."

The boy looked up at him with a look of unmistakable concern. Anders didn't speak Neanderthal, another reason he wished his friend Khazanov were still here. He glanced down and saw what had been occupying Aku's attention: an impression in the mud. It appeared to be the footprint of a three-toed animal, each toe splayed slightly apart from the other.

Aku flapped his arms up and down and jerked his head back and forth.

Riese joined them, setting the butt of her spear into the soft ground.

"What's he doing?"

Anders shrugged. "Seems he's trying to describe a set of tracks he just found. I think it's some kind of bird. The three toes are right, but this footprint's way too large."

"Maybe it's an ostrich," she proposed. Riese flapped her arms in an attempt to communicate with Aku. She looked uncharacteristically silly and Aku's eyes lit up at the sight. He exaggerated his own mimicry, baring his teeth and gnashing.

"Yeah, I don't think we're dealing with an ostrich here," Riese finally said, giving up the game of charades once and for all.

A terrifying image popped into Anders' mind and he shook it away.

"What's wrong?" Riese asked, eyeing him strangely.

"I think I know what's got Aku so spooked."

A shriek in the distance echoed through the rainforest. Points of gooseflesh formed on Anders' skin.

"The hell was that?" Riese asked, gripping her spear with both hands.

"Something we'd rather not meet," he replied.

"Sounded like a bird," she said.

Anders pulled Aku to his feet and started back for camp. "It's so much worse than that. Imagine a three-hundred-pound turkey with a beak that could snap your femur like a twig."

179

"Sounds like Big Bird on crack," Riese said, following close behind.

Anders nodded, watching Aku leap over a tree stump with ease. "The textbooks call it *Titanis walleri*. But most people know it simply as the terror bird."

Chapter 36

The three were charging through the rainforest with the single goal of reaching the relative safety of the camp when they entered a thirty-foot clearing. Out in front was the spry little Aku, followed by Riese, with Anders bringing up the rear. Thin rays of sunlight struggled through the oppressive canopy in a rare display of good weather. Was it a positive omen of things to come?

They were no more than halfway through the clearing, hopeful thoughts still surging through Anders' head, when something knocked him clean off his feet and sent him sprawling into a patch of giant ferns. The spear clutched in his left hand left his grasp, tumbling end over end until it disappeared into the brush.

Riese and Aku spun around at once. Anders struggled to gather his bearings. The impact had blurred his vision and in those first few frantic seconds all he could see was the shadow of a large creature, struggling to regain its own balance. His first thought was that the terror bird had heard them sprinting through the jungle and zeroed in on the careless noise they were making, but as his eyes slowly cleared, he saw that he was wrong.

The sabertooth regained its footing and began circling Riese, a low growl emitting from its powerful jaws. Stepping back, she raised her spear in a vain attempt to fend the beast off. It growled and swatted the spear away with ease. She watched it fly from her hands, her face a mask of terror.

"Hey," Anders shouted, rising to his feet and waving his hands over his head to get the creature's attention.

It glanced in his direction for less than a second before returning to Riese.

Aku stood a few feet behind her, also paralyzed with fear. Anders called his name and made a motion with his hand. The boy found him and knew immediately what Anders was asking. The boy threw his spear through the air, forcing Anders to jump and catch it.

Backing away, Riese tripped over an exposed root, landing on her backside, her hands splayed out in front of her.

Anders tightened his grip on the spear and charged the beast, burying the tip between its ribs. If it hadn't considered him a threat before, it certainly did now. It howled in pain and batted him to the ground with a swipe from one of its giant paws.

The sabertooth whirled around to face Anders's prone form, the spear protruding from its side. Blood dripped from the handle.

Anders scrambled backwards, digging in his elbows and the heels of his boots, until his back hit the trunk of a tree. Feet away, Riese was shouting, trying to draw the animal's attention, but it wasn't working. This thing was locked onto Anders and preparing to inflict a killing blow. Its cold dead eyes drew closer and for the first time it revealed the impressive ten-inch length of its canines, teeth it was about to bury into his neck.

182

At first, the rustle of movement in the nearby brush escaped Anders' attention. But it wasn't until the ground trembled and a second blur of motion burst into the clearing that he realized things had gone from bad to worse.

The terror bird had arrived with an ear-shattering screech. At nearly eight feet tall and well over two hundred and fifty pounds, the creature was a terrifying sight to behold. Its plump and wingless body was covered in dark mottled feathers which ended in a fanned gray and brown tail.

The sabertooth swung to face this new threat, roaring and lashing out with its sharp claws. But the cat wasn't trying to defend Anders so much as it was trying to protect its dinner. They were fighting over him the way two alley cats might fight over the fishy contents of a garbage can. How sweet.

The adversaries danced in a circle, jabbing and sidestepping like a pair of heavyweight boxers. His back still pressed against the tree, Anders was transfixed, watching the spectacle in utter amazement. Just then, Aku hopped out from the bushes and pulled on his arm. The last thing he saw as he fled the clearing was the terror bird's beak clamping down on the sabertooth's neck, followed by the sound of snapping bone.

They were a few dozen meters away when Riese ran up and pulled Anders into a hug. "I was sure you were a goner," she said. Barely a second later, she let go, realizing what she'd just done.

From the clearing came the gruesome sounds of flesh being torn and bones crunched. Big Bird was going to town.

"We better get out of here while it's busy having dinner," Anders suggested. They ran, eager for the noises of the jungle to drown out the sickening feast.

Chapter 37

A few miles away, a different kind of meal was in progress. One Dr. Daniel Erwin didn't appreciate one single bit. Vacek, Stills, Castleman and Halloway were in the midst of sorting through the plants and rainforest vegetables he'd collected, eating what they could and tossing aside the rest. They slurped and belched with all the grace of men who'd been stranded at sea for weeks.

Castleman pulled his face out of a horned cucumber. Green goo dripped from his chin. "I never knew rabbit food could taste so good."

Stills nodded with enthusiasm as he swallowed down a handful of *Grewia* fruit. "Tell me about it. I was so hungry I coulda eaten an entire chicken, beaks and feet, even their fingernails."

"Chickens don't have fingernails, you idiot," Vacek corrected him. "They have talons, and I'm sure you wouldn't want to feel those coming out your ass."

The men all burst into laughter, except for Erwin, who watched as the four mercs made short work of hours of foraging.

In his mind, he was replaying Vacek's barbed comment over and over again. They wouldn't last a day, he'd yelled, or something to that effect. But on the contrary—and much to Erwin's own surprise—he'd done just fine. As it turned out, the mercs had been the ones in trouble. Seemed the moment the scientists had stripped them of their precious gadgets and prefab foods, they hadn't a clue what to do.

After nearly impaling him on a mammoth's tusk, Vacek had kicked Erwin to his feet, the others ripping off his pack and tearing through it the way thieves might tear through a stolen purse.

It was an image he needed to keep fresh in his mind because no matter how irate he became over the theft of his property, his life was in their hands. A single word from Vacek might be all that stood between him and a sudden, rather painful demise. But the situation wasn't quite that simple, was it? Erwin was no longer a useless mouth to feed. In a harsh environment devoid of MREs and grocery stores, the responsibility for maintaining food stores would fall on him. He alone had the power to deny these men sustenance and by extension allow them all to perish from hunger. But there was another option, wasn't there?

Castleman lifted Erwin's pack, bouncing it up and down to gauge the weight of what was left.

"One more of those cucumber things each before we're out," he said with a hint of concern. The notion of moderation to a group of starving men was about as foreign a concept as table manners.

All eyes turned to Erwin.

185

"You're gonna need to forage again before we head out," Vacek told him, licking the juice off his fingers one by one.

Erwin rose to his feet and stretched his legs, realizing only afterward how much he looked like a sprinter about to run a hundred-meter dash.

"Castleman," Vacek called out. "Go with him and if he tries anything funny…" He drew his dirty thumb across his neck.

Castleman grinned, a glob of green cucumber goo still on his chin.

The mercenaries' failure to catch even a rodent since they'd escaped only reinforced Erwin's conviction that these guys might be skilled at firing weapons, but they were useless once you took away their toys.

He and Castleman trudged through the rainforest, always sure to stay within a hundred feet of the camp. Rather quickly, Erwin spotted a patch of cucumbers and stooped to plop them in the pack Castleman held open. In they went, followed closely behind by Castleman's greedy hand. All those muscles required one hell of an appetite. Erwin would need to work fast.

Shortly after, Erwin spotted a tree with wild nuts and threw them into the pack. Just like before, Castleman scooped up a handful and popped them into his mouth.

"Hmm, those were good. Look for more like that, would you?"

Erwin sighed. This guy was driving him crazy. At this rate they'd be done by noon tomorrow.

When they passed an outcropping of ancient philodendrons, Erwin froze.

"What's the problem?" Castleman demanded.

"Oh, nothing," Erwin lied. "I'm simply not sure how much of this plant to pick. The sweet taste can be addictive."

186

To those knowledgeable in botany, the concentrated toxicity of even a drop of ancient philodendrons' sap was well known. In fact, it was only a few days ago that he'd saved Riese from suffocating to death as she'd tried to drink from one.

"Don't discriminate, Doc. Throw it in and we'll risk the addiction."

Erwin broke off three large leaves and shoved them into the open pack.

He worked slowly from there on out, hoping that Castleman's hunger and curiosity might get the better of him. If the merc gave into temptation and ate the plant, his nearly instantaneous death might give Erwin a good chance of escape.

But it wasn't to be. They collected a few more edibles when Vacek's booming voice ordered them back.

Vacek rose as they strode into camp. "I hope for your sake that you've been straight with us," Vacek said, Stills and Halloway were standing on either side of him.

Erwin felt the muscles in his belly tense. "Course I have."

The leader's eyes flicked between him, Castleman and the backpack. Vacek produced a sharpened stick the height of his shoulders and the thickness of a man's thumb. "People have a funny way of talking, don't they?" the merc leader said, asking no one in particular.

"They sure do," Castleman said, flashing a set of impossibly white teeth.

"Sometimes you talk to folks, using what you think are perfectly normal words," Vacek continued. "Then you start to listen to what you're saying. 'Toe the line,' or 'I'm gonna read you the riot act.' Funny expressions we use every day and we have no idea where they came from. My all-time favorite is 'rule of thumb.'" His eyes found Erwin's and they were gleaming. "You familiar with that one, doc?"

Erwin hesitated before nodding slowly. "I've heard of it."

"Goes back to an English judge from the seventeen hundreds named Sir Francis Buller." Vacek moved the sharpened stick from one hand to the other. "Story goes, a man was brought before his court, charged with beating his adulterous wife. Sir Francis listened to both sides carefully before ruling that it was a husband's right to beat his wife, so long as the stick he used was thinner than his thumb."

Erwin swallowed hard.

"So let me make myself perfectly clear. I'm gonna ask you a question and if I don't get the truth I won't be nearly as kind as Francis Buller. Fact, I'll ram this spear so far up your ass you'll be tasting wood for a month."

"What do you wanna know?" Erwin asked, certain Vacek somehow knew about his secret plan.

"The metal case you stole, where is it?"

"Oh, that," Erwin said, genuinely surprised.

Standing by Vacek's left shoulder, Castleman glared at him as he reached into the bag and pushed an ancient philodendron stem into his mouth.

"Don't eat that," Erwin shouted, batting it out of the black mercenary's hand.

Stills swung out with lightning speed, knocking Erwin off his feet with an open fist to his chest.

"The hell are you—" Castleman started to say before his speech slurred and his eyes fired wide with fright. Strange guttural sounds emanated from his throat as his hands clamped around his neck, tearing at the collar of his shirt in a desperate attempt to breathe. For their part, his comrades were at a complete loss, shouting at their friend to tell them what was wrong.

And for a precious few seconds, as their attention shifted from Erwin to the stricken Castleman, he knew it was now or never. In one swift motion, he snatched the pack off the ground and tore into the jungle, running with the legs of a man who would be gutted in the worst possible way if they ever managed to catch him.

Erwin hadn't covered more than ten yards before he caught the distinctive sound of at least two sets of feet charging through the jungle after him. He scurried over a fallen tree and down a steep slope replete with thick vines protruding up from the ground in a veiled conspiracy to trip him. After narrowly avoiding that particular obstacle, Erwin's boot landed in a three-foot patch of mud. That sent him to the ground in an involuntary and excruciating version of the splits.

Rolling over, he fought to get to his feet, but not before he felt a kick to the abdomen from Vacek's boot. Erwin's body was sent nearly a foot into the air from the blow, the air knocked clean out of his lungs.

"Don't kill me," he begged his tormentors, coughing and fighting to regain his breath.

Vacek raised the spear over his head, his face a mask of pure rage.

"Your silver case," Erwin squealed. "Don't kill me and I'll show you where it is."

The spear thudded into the soft earth next to Erwin's head. He lay on his back, his chest heaving, wondering how many more hours of life he'd managed to buy himself.

Chapter 38

Five miles to the north, Anders, Riese and the others came to a stop next to a stream. Water filled with sediment rushed over slime-covered boulders. They hadn't stopped hoofing it through the rainforest since the sabertooth and terror bird had tried to make a lunch out of them. Thirst and exhaustion were beginning to set in. Binh bent down with the last remaining filter bottle, intent on refilling it.

"Hold up," Anders shouted.

Binh stopped and regarded his friend curiously.

"Water's too full of sediment," Anders told him. "The only thing you'll do is clog our one remaining bottle."

Binh's eyes were fixated on Anders' chest. Barely visible beneath his torn blue coveralls were four red lines where the sabertooth had raked him with its claws.

Binh hollered, giving him shit for not saying anything sooner.

"Stop worrying," Anders said. "I'm fine."

Riese opened his coverall and let out a sigh. "Stop trying to be a hero," she scolded him. "This looks like it's starting to get infected."

"We've got to keep moving," Anders said, checking his watch and seeing they had less than thirty-five hours to get back with the vaccine.

Ignoring him, she turned to Jim, who had made the decision to join them rather than take his chances with the terror bird.

"Any chance you have something we can use to disinfect these cuts?" she asked. Her eyes dropped to the hack job he'd done on his Genesis uniform. "Never mind."

Binh pointed into the brush and spoke.

"He says he might be able to mix together a salve to hold off infection," Anders said with a touch of hope.

"He said all that?" Riese asked. "I didn't think he spoke that long."

Anders rolled his eyes. "More or less. When you've been friends for as long as Binh and I, you don't need much to know what the other guy's gonna say."

Her eyes fell to the rushing water as Binh and Jim headed off.

"What is it?" Anders asked.

"Oh, nothing," Riese said. "It's just, you two are close."

Anders closed his coverall. "Maybe, but Binh and I are about as different as two men get. Somehow it works."

"Sounds silly, but I've just never had a friend like that."

Anders laughed and then winced from the pain. "Know what your problem is, Riese?" he said.

She stared up at him. "No, but something tells me I'm about to find out."

"Your castle walls are too high and your moat's too deep." He watched her digest the comment.

She rinsed her hands in the cool water, smiling. "Are you quoting some sort of bro code manual?"

"It means sometimes you gotta take a chance and let people in."

She picked up a twig and tossed it, watching the river sweep it away.

The sounds of the jungle filled the open space. For the first time since they'd left Jim's camp, Aku was nowhere to be seen. The kid could pull off one hell of a disappearing act. David Copperfield would have been jealous.

"He'd do anything for you, you know," she said after a moment.

"Who, Binh?" Anders replied.

"Yeah. How'd the two of you meet?"

Anders smiled at the memory. "A poker game on a river boat along the Chao Phraya River. There were five of us. Less than an hour in, the pot was piled high with more than just chips. Gold teeth, expensive clothes, even the keys to a commercial fishing boat. I had pocket fives with two more on the flop. The turn and river both came up queens and Binh bet. I raised, knowing by the smug look on his face he was holding ladies full of fives. He went all in after that, confident of victory. I flicked over my cards. When he saw my four of a kind, all the blood drained from his face. I scooped my winnings into my shirt and was getting ready to head out when an irate Vietnamese woman stormed in, shouting at the man seated next to me. Only after the two exchanged some choice words did I find out that man was Binh. Turns out earlier in the evening he'd gambled away the family home and she was threatening to divorce his sorry ass. The scene gave everyone around a good laugh, but I

192

didn't think it was funny, especially when she starting asking what would become of their six kids.

"Listen, a win's a win, but I guess you could say I took pity on the guy. I gave him back what he lost, along with the gold teeth, which were his. Even gave him the shirt, along with a handful of chips. Must have had a moment of weakness, that's how I explained it to myself at the time. But I did keep the boat and renamed it the *Lady Luck*. Still have it. I reckon it's somewhere off the coast of Portugal, only twelve thousand years in the future."

Riese's hand touched his and he pretended not to notice.

"What about his kids?" she asked. "Did they end up going to school?"

"Binh's kids were never in danger."

"What?" she said, retracting her hand. "But I thought you said—"

"I found out later it was all a lie. The woman wasn't Binh's wife. She was a local prostitute he'd paid to show up in case he lost."

"That little scam artist." Riese looked visibly upset.

Anders only laughed. "Soon as I found out, I hired him on the spot and we've been besties ever since."

Now it was Riese's turn to giggle. "Besties?"

"What?"

She waved him away. "I just haven't heard that from a grown man before. Teenage girl, yes."

Anders leaned in. "I think you'll find I'm full of surprises."

She didn't back away and, seeing that, he came in even closer. A surge of electricity ran up his legs and out his fingers. He felt light and giddy. Their lips touched for barely a second when a branch snapped. He looked over to find Aku parked by a tree, staring at them, grinning widely.

193

"Get outta here, you little perv," Anders shouted, tossing a stone. It struck the tree next to him and Aku ran off.

"Now where were we?" he asked, swiveling back to Riese, only to find her no longer there.

She was over by the river's edge, pretending to fix her clothes. Anders swore under his breath right as Binh and Jim returned, bearing gifts.

•••

Binh mixed the antibacterial paste in a large green leaf while Anders sat watching with a look of consternation. The recipe consisted mainly of traditional Chinese medicine with a Boatese twist.

"Remind me what's in this crazy concoction of yours?" Anders asked, watching his friend work the ingredients with the flattened end of a stick.

Binh told him.

"Pangolin scales and *Radix bupleuri?*" Anders repeated with added unease. "I don't know, doesn't anyone have some good old-fashioned antibiotics?"

Riese was nearby, studying the display of her handheld DNA sequencer. She'd been ignoring him ever since the others had returned, her eyes glued to that little gizmo.

Binh stood up and walked over, cupping the giant leaf that contained a brown gooey substance. Anders caught one whiff and jerked away.

"Oh, for the love of God, that stuff smells awful. I'm starting to consider taking my chances with infection."

Binh flashed that winning smile and told Anders to sit still and open his coverall. Reluctantly, Anders did as he was told, wincing from the sharp sting as Binh began rubbing in the paste. He tried to think of it as Vicks VapoRub, but made from forest turds.

194

"Does this horrible thing have a name?" he asked, eager for Binh to be done.

Binh said he didn't know, but told him what it was designed to treat.

"Bacterial vaginosis?" Anders shouted. "Are you trying to kill me?"

Binh explained that it was the only antibacterial recipe he knew.

Anders rose to his feet and carefully buttoned up his coverall. "You're getting even with me for something, aren't you?"

Binh threw up his hands, covered in brown paste, pleading his innocence.

Just then Jim burst into the small clearing and skidded to a stop, favoring his sore ankle. "I was scouting ahead," he said. Still out of breath, he poked a hand into his pocket, plucked out a white bulbous larva and popped it into his mouth.

Riese and Anders cringed. Binh held his hand out for one.

"I came to an open field," Jim said, spreading out his arms. "Admiring the view when I looked up and saw the horizon was nothing but a big patch of blue."

"The Mediterranean?" Anders asked, hopeful.

Jim nodded vigorously. "Yeah, and no more than a mile or two from here." He paused, his nose twitching. "What's that horrible smell?"

"Don't ask," Anders said as they set about gathering their things together.

Then from out of the forest came a nerve-shattering screech, one Anders was intimately familiar with. His body tensed. The others froze in place.

The terror bird had finished its sabertooth snack and was looking for dessert.

Chapter 39

Less than a mile away, Vacek planted his feet, listening intently to the shriek as it echoed through the jungle. His right hand tensed around the shaft of the wooden spear. Whatever that was, it sounded mighty pissed.

"How far away, you think?" Stills asked. Beads of sweat dotted his smooth milky scalp.

"Hard to say," Vacek whispered back. "But far too close for comfort."

The four of them were trailing Anders and the other members of his ragtag group north. They were heading for the sea and that was exactly where Vacek hoped to catch them, with their backs to the water and nowhere left to run.

With no military or survival training, the scientists shouldn't have lasted this long. Discovering Erwin with a pack stuffed with edible plants when Vacek and his men were starving had been a tremendous blow to his ego. He'd expected—or hoped—to find most of the civilians dead or at least curled into a ball, racked with hunger and dehydration. No doubt about it, there was an 'I told you so' moment in there, and he'd been the one forced to eat humble pie.

For the last few hours, with the readout on his OLED display bugging in and out, Vacek had opted to power it off and track them the old-fashioned way. There was something exhilarating about reading marks on the ground that no blinking blue dot could ever hope to compete with.

And the tracks he'd found had told him an interesting story. Anders' group had recently met up with someone new. The size and shallow depth of the person's prints gave Vacek with several bits of useful information. For starters, the newcomer was thin and male. But more importantly, he was favoring his right foot, a description which matched what Grieves had said was a lost member from Genesis' earlier mission.

Vacek glanced down at the metal briefcase in his other hand, its smooth surface smeared with mud. Erwin had kept his word and led them to the case. True to his word, Vacek had let him live, at least for now. There would be a reckoning for Castleman's murder. Erwin was still collecting their food, but with one major difference. Before Vacek or his remaining men ate a thing, Erwin was the first to take a bite.

The sound of movement in the bush nearby made Vacek swing his body in that direction. Something was coming directly at them, something that was moving fast.

Erwin backed away from the noise, clutching the side of a thick tree for protection. Spears gripped with both hands, Stills and Halloway dropped to the ground in a low stance, scanning the impenetrable wall of vegetation before them.

To their left stood Vacek. He'd set the briefcase on the ground and tightened the grip on his own spear by using a piece of vine as an improvised strap. If push came to shove, he didn't want to lose a hold on the only weapon he had.

The footsteps grew louder until the terror bird charged through an opening in the brush, knocking Stills and Halloway over like a pair of bowling pins. Halloway's spear flew from his hand and landed somewhere in the thicket. Vacek stumbled backwards, tripping over the briefcase right as Halloway and Stills scrambled back onto their feet. The terror bird skidded to a stop and turned sharply. For the first time they beheld what they were up against.

The creature's curved beak and talons dripped with fresh blood. It lunged out, snapping its massive, orange beak at Halloway and then Stills. Halloway dodged while Stills parried the attack. He stepped back to thrust his spear at the creature when it moved in and tore a chunk of flesh from his chest. Stills howled in pain right as Vacek came charging past him and drove the sharpened point of his spear deep into the terror bird's breast. For a moment, it continued to struggle, but the wound had been a fatal one and the animal's legs gave out, sending it crumpling to the ground.

As it lay dying, Halloway dropped to tend to Stills.

Vacek planted his boot on the terror bird's neck and yanked his spear out.

"Will he live?" Vacek asked Halloway.

Halloway nodded. "Once I manage to stop the bleeding."

"Good, because we're gonna need his engineering skills to repair the stasis chamber."

Erwin came out from behind the tree, looking relieved. "I was sure we were goners," he said, stopping next to the bird and inspecting its bloodstained corpse.

Vacek motioned to the kill. "You know what this means?" he asked Erwin.

The paleobotanist shook his head.

198

Without another word, Vacek buried the spear deep into Erwin's chest. The scientist's eyes bulged and his mouth flapped open in a silent scream. He gripped the spear shaft, a trickle of blood running from his mouth before his body went limp and he collapsed dead.

"Why'd you do that?" Halloway asked, hovering over Stills.

"I did it for Castleman," Vacek told him. "We don't need his rabbit food anymore." He nudged the terror bird with the tip of his spear. "Not when we've got chicken for days."

Chapter 40

Back on the *Excelsior*, Khan was in his office, watching the anchors on CNN convulse with orgasmic delight over the spread of the pandemic. Not that he believed they relished the prospect of misery, but strife was their bread and butter and with the outbreak of a deadly disease, viewership had been at an all-time high. Especially with news that a hundred million cases of infection had been reported with projections expected to reach close to a billion in the coming days. Some in the media had begun referring to it as the Red Death because of the way its victims bled from their eyes and ears. The speed with which the disease spread was unparalleled, making it perhaps the most efficient killing machine in human history, a fact which left Khan unsure whether to feel horrified or awestruck.

The intercom on his desk buzzed, drawing his attention from the newscast. He wasn't worried he would miss anything, since they'd been repeating the same boring scraps of information over and over for the last few days. But as the severity of the situation came into full view, Khan had begun finalizing the plan he hoped might provide worthy members of the human race with a fighting chance at survival. Unfortunately, the first stage was the longest shot of all since it required Vacek's team to reopen transit to Gihon.

He thumbed the red button on his desk. "What is it?"

"It's Mr. Davenport to see you, Mr. Khan," Shirley replied, her voice sounding muffled and strange. "He says it's quite urgent."

"Fine, send him in."

The automatic door swished open and in walked a figure wearing a fully enclosed mask. The sound of a breathing system pushing air in and out made Khan wonder whether a character from some science fiction film was standing before him.

Davenport pulled off the mask and tucked it under his arm.

"I hope you're only being dramatic," Khan said, tapping a button on his desk which muted the bank of televisions on the wall.

"I wish I was," Davenport replied, setting another mask on the table. "I think you should put this on, sir."

"Where's Ms. Meadows?" Khan demanded. If anyone should be barging in here with outlandish orders it was usually her.

"I'm sorry to report that she's in quarantine," Davenport said and Khan couldn't help but notice the tiniest sign of satisfaction in the man's eyes.

"Quarantine?" Even Khan couldn't hide his shock at the news. Davenport's festering hatred for Meadows had started the minute she'd replaced him. But the man's childish animosity was misplaced since it wasn't Meadows who had stolen his position. It was he who had failed to hold onto it.

201

"The virus must've come aboard in one of our Cutters returning from a supply run."

Khan rose to his feet and pressed his palms against the mahogany desk. "You're saying the infection's on the ship?" This was no longer a crisis happening to someone else—this was hitting far too close to home.

"So far, six crew members have fallen ill. Like Meadows, each of them is in quarantine and under observation. Precautions are in place throughout the ship, sir, which is why I suggest you wear this mask. At least until we can ensure we've got things back under control."

"Perhaps it's time we dock and offload the infected," Khan said.

"That's no longer an option, sir," Davenport said, fingers laced in front of him. "The *Excelsior* has been forbidden from docking in any nearby ports."

"Fine, then prep a Cutter," Khan declared. "I'm heading ashore."

Davenport's eyes dropped. "I probably wasn't clear enough, sir. The *Excelsior* and all associated craft have been blacklisted. Even if we dropped you ashore via dinghy, the authorities will know you've come from an infected vessel."

The color rose in Khan's cheeks. "The only way anyone would know who's on board was if you told them."

"By law we were required to provide a manifest as soon as the first case was reported."

Khan let out a humorless laugh. "Always a stickler for the rules," he scoffed. "Exactly the reason I had you replaced. If Meadows was here, she'd have navigated something as trivial as a law whose very purpose was to corral the powerless and the weak."

Davenport wore an appropriate mask of shame for a subordinate who had failed to lie and cheat for his boss.

202

But something about that expression seemed false to Khan. If there had been someone else on board nearly as qualified, Khan would have fired the man on the spot, even sent him to quarantine if possible.

Davenport bowed his head and dismissed himself.

When he was gone, Khan collapsed into his chair.

The curved glass visor of the mask on his desk reflected images from the bank of televisions on the wall. Scenes of upheaval and chaos from around the world. That thin veil of civilization was beginning to shatter.

In a matter of days, he'd gone from one of the most powerful men in the world to little more than a boat person, a prisoner on his own ship. Any hope of salvation now rested squarely with the team they'd sent into the distant past. If they failed to reclaim the colony and restore the link to the present, this ship would become his tomb and the planet little more than a cemetery littered with bones.

Chapter 41

24 hours remaining

The briny smell of the sea hit Anders long before he emerged from the jungle. Then came the deep blue of the Mediterranean, as the fading late afternoon sun drew glittering fingers along the water's surface. They were on high ground with a clear view across the strait, the Rock of Gibraltar in the far distance. Directly ahead lay the southern tip of Spain, although neither would be known by those names for thousands of years to come. During most of the ancient world, this gateway had been referred to as the Pillars of Hercules, so named because they marked the limit of Hercules' westward travels during the discharge of his Twelve Labors.

Binh tapped Anders' shoulder and pointed to a sight below them that nearly stole his breath away. A bustling port city, lined with beige buildings, laid out in a grid.

From the center rose a tall obelisk, flanked by a series of what appeared to be temples and government buildings.

A steady stream of small sailing ships plied their way in and out of port.

"Xanbar," Jim said, unable to keep from smiling at the beautiful sight.

In the history books, the modern city of Tangier was said to have been founded by the Carthaginians sometime in the fifth century BCE. Surveying Xanbar, situated as it was in the very same spot, Anders knew modern archaeologists were off once again, this time by more than a few millennia.

A winding trail led down from the heights overlooking the city. As they descended, rectangular patches of farmland stretched away from the city walls. Tending to the crops were dozens, maybe hundreds of squat and muscular-looking men and women wearing little more than loin cloths made from animal skins.

Men armed with swords patrolled the area, riding bareback on white horses. Anders quickly realized the men and women cultivating the crops were wearing chains.

"Do you think they're slaves or prisoners?" Riese asked, sounding pained.

"Six of one, half a dozen of the other," Jim replied.

In other words, it didn't make an ounce of difference, although a prisoner could hope for freedom after serving his sentence, whereas a slave's plight was usually for life.

As they reached the dirt road which led toward the main gate, Anders noticed something else about the workers—their foreheads and torsos bore a distinct shape. "I guess there's no more doubt about how they're using the Neanderthals they've been capturing."

Riese took a closer look, careful not to draw too much attention. "You're right."

205

The city gate was open and they moved into the city, merging with the growing traffic of donkey-drawn carts and groups of travelers. More than likely there were other cities along the coast and roads for those too poor to pay for voyage by sea, all an unlikely network which had developed with the emergence of Gihon.

Trekking down the dusty streets, Anders was in utter amazement at what he saw. The clothing these people wore was fascinating. Some looked ancient Egyptian—men with light-fitting wraparound skirts known as shendyts, women in simple sheath dresses called kalasirises. But not everyone looked alike. Others were garbed in what could only be considered Mayan clothing—colorfully textured woolen ponchos draped over the body and accompanied by a similar set of slacks.

On their feet nearly all of them wore what appeared to be wooden sandals, bound to the foot and sometimes the leg with thin strips of leather.

While the archaeological side of Anders' brain was doing backflips, Riese made a rather interesting observation.

"I'm surprised no one's staring at us," she said, glancing around.

Anders passed a woman who plugged her nose as they walked by. "Speak for yourself."

Binh reminded them they'd just spent days in the jungle and probably smelled horrible.

"Some of us stink worse than others," Anders said, indicating the eye-watering goop Binh had lathered onto his chest. Not only that, their faces and clothing were covered in dried mud.

A Cutter roared overhead and settled down in a landing zone out of sight. Anders had been watching it come in when he bumped into a man in a yellow jumpsuit with a Genesis logo on his chest. The two stared intently at one another as they crossed paths. When he was gone, Anders turned back to the others.

"I guess that explains why we don't look so out of place," he told them.

"We better hurry up and find passage to Gihon as quickly as possible," Jim said.

Riese pointed to where the Cutter landed. "Then shouldn't we head to the landing pad and talk to one of the pilots?"

Jim shook his head. "I'm not sure that's such a good idea. As far as Lacroix is concerned, we're the enemy."

"Far as I'm concerned, he can keep his damn island," Riese protested. "I just want that vaccine and a ticket home."

"I think Jim's right," Anders said. "Once he realizes we've been sent here by Genesis, we may lose more than a trip back to the present. I think our best bet is to ditch these clothes and hire passage on a boat."

The muscles in Riese's mud-splattered face fell flat and Anders couldn't help marvel that even after being dragged through the wringer these last few days, she still looked beautiful.

"We cram ourselves onto one of those dinky sailboats and we're likely to end up at the bottom of the sea," she said.

Anders curled his thumbs under his life vest. "That's where your vest comes in."

Binh's was gone and he let that fact be known.

"Don't worry, buddy," Anders said. "We'll find you something else."

They followed the flow of human traffic cluttering the streets and soon found themselves in a market. In the center stood the obelisk they'd spotted from the hills overlooking Xanbar.

A man nearby stood on a small wooden platform, waving his arms and beckoning people in. Meanwhile, a line of Neanderthals in chains were led on stage with him.

"Oh, goodness," Riese said, covering her mouth with disgust. "We just walked into a slave auction."

The master of ceremonies motioned to each of the Neanderthal captives, seeming to play up their broad arms and powerful legs. Guards armed with swords and whips stood on stage with them, ready to strike at any of the slaves who stepped out of line.

"I can't watch this," Riese said, turning away.

Anders couldn't blame her. He pointed to a collection of clothing vendors they had passed on their way into the market. "Binh, take Jim and get us some fresh clothes. Something we can use to blend in once we reach the island."

Binh stuffed his hands into his pockets and pulled out the lining to show he had no money.

Anders thought for a moment and then removed his watch. "Take this," he said, holding it out before hesitating for a moment.

Binh still looked uncertain.

"You're Boatese," Anders chided him. "You know how to barter, don't you?"

Binh snatched the watch and shook his head with a look of disdain.

"And don't get me anything dumb-looking," Anders shouted back as he and Riese left.

From there he and Riese headed toward the wharf to see if they could charm their way aboard a ship. The streets of Xanbar were less busy with the slave auction in full swing.

As they moved along, Anders studied the two-story stone and mud brick buildings. Esthetically they were simple square structures framed with small windows designed to keep out the heat.

"Take a look at that," Riese said, indicating an imposing statue being erected nearby.

It depicted a man in a modern-looking suit, his head adorned with a Panama hat. Curled majestically at his feet was a pet lion.

"Who's this?" Riese asked.

Anders furrowed his brow. "My best guess is you're looking at the face of Gihon's new leader."

"There's something I've been meaning to ask you," she said, her eyes narrowing thoughtfully as she watched the men chisel away. "What happens when you throw a rock in a pond?"

Anders' brow scrunched up. "This sounds like one of those Taoist koans. What is the sound of one hand clapping?"

She slapped his shoulder. "Can you be serious for a minute? I'm talking about small actions in the past having a knock-on effect in the future."

They continued walking. "What about it?"

"Well, these Cutters we see flying around and the men in orange jumpsuits walking the streets. Don't you think any of this will create a problem? Am I the only one who's worried that their irresponsibility might completely alter the future?"

Anders thought about it for a second. "Recorded history, which is to say the bits of the past we have in written form, won't take shape for at least another five thousand years with the Ancient Sumerians in Mesopotamia and the Ancient Egyptians." Anders glanced over his shoulder and then grabbed Riese's hand in alarm. "But I'll tell you what does worry me."

She tracked the movement of his eyes. "What is it?"

Already Anders' heart was starting to hammer in his chest. "I think we're being followed."

Chapter 42

Two men stood watching them from the mouth of a shaded alleyway, both dressed in blue security uniforms. The one on the left with the short-cropped blond hair whispered into the cuff of his shirt. The other, a dark-haired man with a beard, fished a pair of black leather gloves from his back pocket and slid them on.

"Keep moving," Anders told her as they continued past a beggar in rags eagerly banging a dirty plastic cup on the ground.

The mishmash of old and new was playing with Anders' mind.

"I can see the masts of the ships," Riese said, indicating where they protruded above the tops of the low buildings. "The pier isn't far from here."

Anders and Riese broke into a run, and so too did the men pursuing them. Clearly this was not simply the result of an overactive imagination, as Anders had hoped.

The crowds grew denser as they got closer to the docks.

"Head right," he said, shoving her into a shaded alley.

"Hey," she shouted. "That hurts."

They landed in the doorway of a small apartment block. The smell of human waste was strong here and Riese covered her nose. Kids ran back and forth, playing in the muck. He nudged her far enough into the doorway that they could see the bustling street without the risk of being seen themselves.

Anders watched the two men pursuing them run by. He was holding her tight. "I think we're okay." He glanced down until their eyes met.

"That's good. Then you can let go of me."

He smiled. "And if I don't want to?"

"Then I'll yell and have you arrested."

There was a playful glint in her sharp blue eyes. Staring into them, Anders couldn't help feeling a little lost, like a boy with a dumb crush.

"You'd miss me too much."

"Try me."

He gently cupped the back of her head and pulled her in for a kiss. She didn't resist. Far from it, her body grew limp as their lips touched. Part of him had expected a hard shove followed by a string of profanities, but that never came. Instead, Riese slid her arms around his neck and swung him around, his back slamming hard against the opposite wall. They were in someone's kitchen, their blind hands knocking over empty ceramic bowls and cups, their lips exploring each other's mouths with pent-up passion. Riese was clearly the aggressor now, berating him as she kept him pinned in place.

"You're such an asshole, you know that?" she said, breathing heavily.

He kissed her hard and then broke away.

211

"And you're a cold, stuck-up—"

The woman's shriek startled both of them. In a flash, Anders and Riese came apart to a fat woman waving her hands at the mess they'd made, shouting in a language they didn't understand. But it didn't take a Khazanov to figure out what she was saying.

Riese struggled to button her one-piece back up while Anders did his best to calm the woman down. They backed out of her home, Anders splaying his hands out in a vain effort to appease her. She followed them into the alley, grabbing a broom on her way out the door and swung it at his head.

"Whoa," he shouted, dodging the blow as he stumbled backwards.

Anders and Riese sprinted through the alley, away from the main road. Thankfully, Xanbar was laid out in a grid pattern, which meant there was more than one way to get to the shipyard.

By the time they emerged from the cool shade of the alley and into the warmth of the sunny street, the crazed woman had given up her pursuit.

Anders started to laugh, his thick hair still disheveled from where Riese had run her fingers through it. She joined in, shaking off little by little that impenetrable wall she liked to surround herself with. He pointed to the docks, which were visible now in the distance, when every muscle in his body began to violently convulse. Electrified pain shot from the top of his head to the tips of his toes. He wanted to scream but he couldn't and he had a good idea why.

He'd been shot with an inhibitor. Keeling over, his body a single rigid structure, Anders heard Riese scream as she tried in vain to fight off their assailants. After that, he felt rough hands on him before the world went black.

Chapter 43

Anders came to with the throbbing pain of a migraine, his vision a blurry mess. In the background was the drone of thrusters. They were in a Cutter, Riese sitting beside him, hands zip-tied, her face a mask of worry and anger. Across from them were the two security men they'd seen following them earlier.

"How are you, Dr. Anders?" the bearded man asked. He was polite for a guy who'd nearly killed him.

"I feel like someone who threw a keg party and decided not to share."

The bearded man grinned knowingly. "It'll pass." The security man's eyes dropped to his nails. "Used to bite them down to nubs," he said. "A nasty habit."

"So's killing billions of innocent people." Anders was referring to the people in the twenty-first century, dying from the virus, but he might as well have included the hundreds or even thousands of test subjects they'd tortured.

The bearded man curled his fingers into tight fists, his knuckles making a popping sound as he did so. "You've been misinformed, Dr. Anders. We're saving people, but I don't expect you to understand that, not yet."

The smug look on his bearded face made Anders yearn to tear him a new and far less flattering look.

The man studied the tense muscles in Anders' arms with dark eyes. "Save your strength. We're nearly there."

Anders let his head relax against the cabin wall, allowing the vibrations from the aircraft frame to soothe his aching head. The porthole window looked out onto an expanse of water. It was noticeably different from the turquoise color of the Mediterranean that surrounded Xanbar. This was darker, deeper.

They were high enough that he could see the slight curvature of the earth.

Before long, the Cutter began to descend and Anders swallowed to alleviate the pressure building in his ears.

Slowly, an object began to form in the vast expanse of flinty water beneath them. Soon, they approached an island roughly five square miles in size with high mountain peaks, the majority of which was covered with lush forest. They'd dropped to about ten thousand feet before Anders spotted what looked like an oddly-shaped city next to the coastline. It appeared to be composed of a series of concentric rings, just as it had been described in Plato's work.

The sight sent chills dancing up his spine.

Gradually, buildings began to take shape, a blend of structures both modern and ancient nestled side by side. More buildings lead away from the circular port area into the mountains, some perched precariously along outcroppings of rock. The window fogged up and Anders realized his jaw was hanging open in utter amazement. Ships on sea as well as in the air flowed in and out of the city like blood cells traveling through major arteries in the human body. The Ancient Egyptians might have referred to such a place as Aaru; to

214

the Greeks Elysium, the Norse would have called it Valhalla. But to Anders, Atlantis seemed just as good a name as any.

Chapter 44

Once the Cutter set down, Anders and Riese were led up a flight of stone steps toward a majestic domed building that would have looked more at home in fifth-century Constantinople than as a corporate research outpost. Framing the impressive structure were a series of ragged peaks dotted with lush vegetation and cascading waterfalls.

They were in some sort of fairy tale, Anders was certain of it. It was the Atlantis he'd spent most of his career searching for, but not the one he'd expected to find.

As they scaled the steps, the city slowly came into view. Several parts were still under construction and even there the modern and ancient were thoroughly intertwined. Mechanical excavators dug into the ground right next to gangs of chained Neanderthals shifting mounds of earth or carrying supplies. The social hierarchy here was clear and it followed evolutionary lines. Just as in Xanbar, *Homo sapiens* oversaw them. But the ultimate wardens were the men and women wearing company coveralls and carrying a variety of modern weapons.

The hot sun seared the top of Anders' head and shoulders as they climbed each riser. Finally, he, Riese and the two guards escorting them passed through a high archway and into a cavernous chamber, their footfalls echoing with each step. Inside, the air was cool and refreshing. The only furniture in sight was a single desk and chair, both ornately decorated. Seated there busy at work was a man in a crisp white suit and a matching Panama hat. Lying at his feet was a young lion bound by a thick chain.

They were only a few feet away when the man glanced up at them. His facial structures hinted at European ancestry—Belgian or French. His accent confirmed it.

"Welcome to Gihon," the man said, that first word sounding to Anders like 'well-cume'.

With a flourish, he snatched a cane dangling from the edge of the desk and sprang to his feet. "Dr. Anders, Dr. Riese," he said, nodding to each of them in turn. "My name is Phillipe Lacroix. You might say that I'm the current custodian of this little slice of heaven." He stared at them intently. Deep grooves along the edges of his eyes and nose revealed his age to be somewhere in his mid-fifties. "I can see that both of you are still in quite a bit of shock," he said, "but don't worry, it will wear off soon enough. That's one of the marvelous things about the human race, don't you think? Our ability to adapt. With time, even the extraordinary becomes ordinary once again."

"We've come for the vaccine," Anders said, cutting through the pleasantries.

217

Lacroix's expression shifted, turning curious, almost confused. "Vaccine?" he asked.

Anders swallowed hard, but Riese spoke before he had a chance.

"I'm sure you're already aware that the pathogen ravaging the twenty-first century is threatening to wipe the entire human race off the planet in the next fifteen hours unless we can stop it."

Lacroix nodded. "Oh, believe me, I'm quite familiar with Pyrenean hemorrhagic fever and its origins. There was something of a vaccine being developed, but it was destroyed, along with all the research."

"Why would you do such a thing?" Riese asked, horrified.

"The entire program was an abomination and needed to be eradicated. You may not understand now, but you will soon enough. Besides, I know the real reason Mr. Khan sent you back."

"The real reason?" Riese asked, clearly still reeling from the news they'd come all this way for something that no longer existed.

"Of course. How else do you think I knew your names? It's the very reason you weren't killed outright. You aren't assassins, although you were hired to help guide them here."

"Not knowingly," Anders interjected.

Nudging his pet lion cub by the leash, Lacroix headed for the stairs, the others following close behind. "Gihon could use people with your particular talents," he told them.

There was an awkward pause as Anders wondered whether he had known about the extent of Vacek's plans to destroy the island. "Wait a minute. Are you saying you don't have a vaccine?"

"What I am saying," Lacroix said, enunciating each word, "is that you and your colleagues have been led on

218

a fool's errand." His eyes fell to the cane in his hand and then back to them. "Khan didn't tell you, did he?"

"Tell us what?" Riese asked. There was fear in her voice and not just because their lives were in danger. She was afraid of what Lacroix was about to say.

"One year ago, the leaders of the developed world held a secret summit in order to discuss a rather troublesome dilemma they were having." Holding his hands out flat, he touched both of his fingers together and slowly lifted them till they were level with his chest. "Over the last few decades, melting ice sheets have meant rising water levels and diminishing landmass. Every year tens of millions living along poor coastal regions are displaced and many of them are now cramped in cargo ships clogging the port cities of the world's richest nations. The ships were meant to be temporary accommodation, but instead they have become floating ghettoes where a whole new society has taken hold. You refer to these unfortunate souls as boat people."

"I don't understand what this has to do with any of that," Anders said. The zip tie restraining his hands had officially begun cutting off his circulation.

"I might," Riese whispered, disbelief on her face. "But I'm hoping like hell that I'm wrong."

Lacroix smiled. "In their infinite wisdom, the assembled leaders decided to rid themselves of the nuisance once and for all. If the planet's available land was shrinking, then so too should her population.

"But you see, politicians, even ones this powerful, are terrified of bad press. You might say they fear it the way a vampire fears the light. They couldn't very well deport the boat people or march them off to what would inevitably been seen as death camps.

"With this in mind, a secret resolution among nations called for the creation of a virus to be introduced into the various boat people populations. But the virus needed certain characteristics. Originally, it was not intended to kill its victims, since that would have been far too gruesome and potentially dangerous to the rest of the world. Instead, it needed to spread rapidly, attacking the victim's reproductive organs, with the goal of rendering them sterile. Those who were commissioned with creating the virus would also be tasked with providing a vaccine. They knew that somewhere along the line mistakes would occur. Some level of cross-contamination was inevitable. The vaccine would act as their insurance card, one administered only to populations deemed worthy."

"While whole communities were left to wither away."

Lacroix nodded. "It wasn't nearly as dramatic as sending them off to the gas chambers, but it was certainly more efficient and no doubt effective."

Anders turned to Riese. "Is creating a virus like that even possible?"

She nodded. "Nowadays, you can create a virus to do almost anything."

"There's something you're not telling me," Anders said, noticing she was holding something back.

Riese bit her lip. "I heard rumors that our lab had been approached for a top-secret government project, but that we'd turned it down. My supervisor claimed a delegation from the UN had arrived looking for a way to exterminate a select segment of the population, but at the time none of us took the rumor seriously."

Anders turned back to Lacroix in disbelief. "So Genesis said yes."

"And did so eagerly," Lacroix added. "From there, things progressed quickly. The virus creation process was relatively straightforward, but during trials problems emerged. The virus began to mutate. Hosts began to die and those who lived were left sterile. You see, when I joined the company, I believed a colony in the past would provide an excellent opportunity to study extinct plant species. Find cures we could never have dreamt of. But soon the orders came down about what was to come, the inhumane intent of the virus and the human testing that was to begin as soon as possible. We had a massive pool of test subjects that no one would ever know about, free of regulation and oversight.

"My role here was as head of security. As a retired colonel with twenty years in the French Foreign Legion, I was more than qualified. But when the virus began to break quarantine in each of the dozen localized research facilities we were running, I could see things were quickly getting out of hand. Large mass graves were dug in Spain and southern France, and thousands of bodies were flown via Cutter to be disposed of.

"At the time, the head of Gihon was Lars Solberg, a tyrant who ordered technicians to stay on site and keep working on a vaccine in spite of the dangers. For some reason, the Neanderthal population had a natural immunity, but since they represented a different species, it was impossible to bridge that gap. Soon, I began hearing reports that test subjects were being thrown into pits still alive. If Solberg hadn't already crossed a line of human decency, he did then.

"The numbers of disgusted employees began to grow quickly. Galvanizing them into action after that was not difficult. But in a way, Solberg was little more than an instrument being wielded by a morally bankrupt civilization. If a man stabs you with a fork, do you blame the fork or the man holding it?"

Anders' head was still reeling. Lacroix had suggested that feeling of being overwhelmed would pass and yet it seemed stronger now than ever.

Lacroix stopped, bent on one knee to rub a scruff of fur on the young lion's chin. "These creatures are worshiped as gods by the indigenous peoples," he said. "As are we. A writer during the twentieth century once said that 'any sufficiently advanced technology is indistinguishable from magic.' The indigenous population stand in awe of our technological prowess, but when all is said and done, what do we have to show for it? Looking forward from this far back in the past," Lacroix went on, "one can only imagine what our species could have achieved with the elapsing of twelve thousand years. What exalted beings might we have become if the people here had all the knowledge of the twenty-first century? But doesn't the creation of this virus and the sorry state of the world prove how far astray we've gone?"

His eyes were alight with either passion or madness and Anders couldn't tell which it was.

Lacroix motioned to the bearded guard. "Garcia, remove their restraints. We wouldn't want our guests' hands turning purple and falling off, now would we?"

When Garcia was done, Lacroix took a few steps before glancing back. "Well, aren't the two of you coming?"

"Coming where?" Riese wondered, her eyes glassy, as though she were in a dream.

"There's something I need to show you," Lacroix said.

"And what might that be?" Anders asked, trying to get the feeling back in his hands.

"The future, Dr. Anders. I'm about to show you the future."

Chapter 45

He brought them first to a glass-encased pyramid thirty feet high. He explained that it was an experimental greenhouse that appeared to exhibit several benefits over traditional greenhouses. Among them were an increase in the size of the vegetables as well as the speed with which they grew. Lacroix claimed that seeds stored inside the structure demonstrated a forty-five percent increase in yield. There were other claims, and each one stretched credulity more than the last.

Lacroix's objective seemed to be to show off how self-sufficient the colony had become. That far from hurting them, severing ties with Genesis had only made them stronger.

Inside the pyramid structure, men and women in colored jumpsuits tended to rows of crops. There were three such structures, he told them, with plans to add more. Anders noticed the patches on the shoulders of the jumpsuits were different than the coveralls he and Riese were wearing. It appeared that Genesis' corporate image of a crescent moon with a double helix had been replaced with that of a phoenix rising from a heap of ashes. Lacroix hadn't just replaced Lars Solberg, he'd started a revolution with himself as its exalted messiah. But what surprised Anders even more was the broken English and olive skin of the young hydroponics technicians.

"You've been training the local population, haven't you?" he stammered in amazement. Had Lacroix not told them the indigenous people were superstitious, perceiving Genesis employees as gods?

"You see, the secret is to get them young," Lacroix explained. "Once they reach twenty, their worldview has already become too rigid for our purposes. Look at how quickly children in our own time take to the same technology that leaves their parents dazed and confused. The science is unambiguous. Young brains are far more adaptable. But believe me when I say, 'you ain't seen nothing yet.'"

Next, he led them past a water well drilled deep into the island's core. A half-dozen concrete rain-collecting platforms fed the main aquifer hundreds of feet beneath them. There was more water, Lacroix assured them, than they could drink in a lifetime.

"I would be willing to bet you're dying for a nice hot shower," he told Riese, who was left practically drooling at the suggestion. "Here in Gihon, we have nearly every amenity you could imagine."

With dreams of showers still running through their heads, they followed Lacroix into what looked like a Greek temple replete with tall white columns. At the far end was the beginnings of a large statue of Lacroix with his pet lion by his side. It was a larger version of the same one they'd seen being carved in Xanbar. Neanderthal slaves in teams of twenty or more dragged sleds piled with heavy blocks of stone. They were all

224

over the island, and everywhere they were subjected to the same brutal working conditions. More than once during the tour, Lacroix had referred to them as his indispensable work force, but it was clear in actuality they were his chattel.

To the left of the monument celebrating Lacroix's greatness, they entered a long passageway and almost at once caught the sharp sound of hammers striking metal. Near the end of the hall, they entered a windowless room lined with rows of workshop tables. Seated before them were dozens of locals in jumpsuits banging away on metal plates.

"They're using tungsten carbide," Lacroix told them with pride. "The plates themselves are made from titanium."

A light flickered on in Anders' head. He stepped forward, glancing over one of the worker's shoulder, and recognized they were creating Mivers' cheat sheets, just like the one Sykes had fished up from his dig site in the Atlantic.

"We aren't only training the locals," Lacroix said. "Each of these plaques contains formulae essential for advancements in science, engineering and agriculture. All we offer is a kickstart and a vision of the end game that awaits. The rest is up to them. Imagine, for instance, if the people of the Middle Ages were given the secrets of electromagnetism or quantum physics."

"I know exactly what would have happened," Anders said before he could shut his mouth. "They'd have built a bomb and destroyed the planet."

Riese threw him a stern look, a look that told him she might actually be buying Lacroix's bullshit.

"A pessimist at heart," Lacroix tisked with noticeable disapproval. "Let's just say we don't share the same point of view."

"Only because you don't know your history."

Lacroix bristled at Anders' boldness, but before he could respond, a man in a dark suit entered the room.

"I'm sorry to bother you, sir," he said, eyeing the others. "But something's come up."

"Don't mind them," Lacroix said, waving his hand in the air. "What seems to be the problem?"

"We've lost contact with one of our Cutters," he said. "It was somewhere over the Pyrenees transporting a cargo of infected bodies from facility twelve when we lost contact."

"What about their transponder?" Lacroix asked.

"We aren't getting any signal. If they've crashed, it may prove impossible to find the wreck site."

Anders leaned into Riese and whispered over the metallic din around them. "Don't you see what's happening?"

She shrugged her shoulders.

"Did your parents never tell you that whispering was rude?" Lacroix said. The man in the dark suit was gone.

Anders straightened. "If you find that crash site, you may be able to stop the epidemic in the future."

"I'm not following you."

"Twelve thousand years from now, hikers in the Pyrenees Mountains near the village of Sallent de Gallego will stumble onto a body frozen in the ice. When those corpses are thawed out for study, it will release the Pyric Hemorrhagic Fever that Genesis created. You recover the infected from the wreck site and you can prevent the infection from spreading in the first place."

Lacroix smiled. "And why would I want to do that?"

A red flush climbed up Anders' neck.

"Because billions of lives are at stake," Riese said.

"I don't think you've been paying attention," Lacroix replied. "Why should I bother fixing a sick and dying world when the future's about to be rewritten?"

226

The two of them stood, trying to digest what Lacroix was telling them.

"There is one final piece to all of this I think you should see. Afterward, I'm confident your minds will be set at ease."

Chapter 46

Ten minutes later they were aboard a Cutter, ten thousand feet in the air, soaring east over the Mediterranean. Beneath them, Anders could make out the occasional tiny outline of a ship or two struggling against the waves. The pilot leaned back and said, "We aren't far now, sir. Few more minutes."

"Very well," Lacroix replied.

Seated in the back was the bearded security man, his hands in his lap, his thumbs rolling over one another in slow, lazy circles.

Riese and Anders stood near the open cockpit, Lacroix at their side.

"It won't be a surprise for any of you to learn that Genesis wants me dead," Lacroix told them. "But it isn't simply to recoup a potential money-making asset."

"Why am I not surprised," Anders said, setting a hand on the copilot's seat to steady himself.

"They've spent billions on Gihon over the years, as you can well imagine."

228

Riese nodded. Her hair was tied into a ponytail and out of her face. "Gihon did seem fairly lavish for a bioresearch lab."

"The island was meant to serve a dual purpose," Lacroix said. "Although it was established as a cutting-edge research facility, Khan quickly realized it provided an additional benefit as an escape pod."

Anders blinked hard. "Come again?"

"A haven, Dr. Anders, a second chance for the wealthy and privileged of a dying planet. Who among us wouldn't trade living in a hell hole for the untarnished beauty you see around you?"

"You're saying in a worst-case scenario, they planned to leave the future and live here permanently?" Riese said. "And we were the ones helping to make that happen?"

Lacroix nodded. "I know it hurts being lied to, but you and your colleagues were pawns, although I'm sure in many ways you already knew that."

Anders was having a hard time deciding who he hated more, Khan or the nutjob standing next to him.

"Surely by now you have also realized you were not the first group Genesis sent back. And though you may not have signed up to be part of a hit squad, that was exactly the company's plan. Kill me, take back the island and if the virus couldn't be controlled, begin sending back those worth saving. The rest would be left to squabble over ever-dwindling tracts of land as they witnessed the next great extinction."

"This keeps getting better all the time," Anders said.

The pilot activated his mic. "Sixty seconds to arrival."

•••

229

Vacek slid the briefcase under the linen cloak he was wearing as the vessel sailed into Gihon's outer harbor. In Xanbar, he and his two remaining men had stolen clothing so they wouldn't stand out dressed in black tactical gear. From there they'd hired a ship to ferry them to the island, promising payment once they arrived.

Of course, they didn't have a dime to pay the captain with. The minute land was in sight, the whole crew had been thrown overboard.

"Quite different seeing it in real life, isn't it?" Stills said, eyeing the twin fifty-foot statues that flanked the mouth of the harbor.

They'd been shown three-dimensional images of Gihon during their secret pre-mission briefing, one the scientists had been excluded from attending. Among the information had been pictures of their target, Phillipe Lacroix, as well as the location of the stasis chamber. As yet, several things still remained unclear. First was the state of the stasis chamber and the equipment inside. Had Lacroix blown it up or somehow disassembled it? Vacek was sure he hadn't for one simple reason. That room contained priceless pieces of modern technology he could never hope to replace now that he was cut off from Genesis and the future.

On a different note, Vacek also wondered whether they still enjoyed the element of surprise. At least some of the scientists had made it to Xanbar, he knew that much. And yet after an extensive search, none of them had been found.

To make matters worse, Vacek had his own men to contend with. On more than one occasion Stills had inquired about the suitcase. In response, Vacek had tried to suggest that it was a mobile lab designed to analyze the well water on the island. Stills seemed to buy the explanation, or at least he'd stopped asking questions. And that told Vacek something else. His cover as an operative for the Epsilon Brotherhood hadn't yet been compromised.

The vessel eased alongside the dock. Stills and Halloway hopped out and lashed her in place.

They walked down the jetty, each with a heavy woolen cloak draped over their fatigues. Before they proceeded any further, Vacek needed to secure some weapons so that once the designated bomb site was located, there would be no one to stop him.

•••

Lacroix let go of the Cutter's handrail long enough to rub his palms together. "I never tire of seeing this." He leaned forward for a better view out the large cockpit window.

Anders and Riese did the same. At first all they saw was the sea and a patch of sandy shoreline. Slowly the sea began to fill with ships and what at first had looked deserted soon became a lush oasis, surrounded by dozens of buildings.

"Where are we?" Riese asked.

"In what will become Egypt," Lacroix responded, a grin easing onto his weathered face. "It was little more than a simple hunter-gatherer outpost when we first made contact. Needless to say, Solberg was in charge then and so our little pilot project was kept secret for years. We landed and were immediately revered as gods. Like Moses atop Mount Sinai, it was with great enthusiasm that the early Egyptians took the first rudimentary knowledge plates. The symbols inscribed were largely universal and depicted in ways we hoped they would understand. No doubt there were problems, oversights and moments clearly lost in translation, errors which later plate iterations sought to correct.

231

"During that first visit they were given seeds and shown how to plant and grow the crops. We sent them off with knowledge and an image burning in their mind's eye. An image of technological utopia. Like those puffed-up house painters during the Renaissance, it was an image they would spend the rest of their lives trying to emulate."

Anders looked on with amazement as thousands of workers in batches of hundreds and thousands brought large blocks of stone on wooden rollers to carvers, already busy shaping a large chunk of limestone. Although not complete, the shape of the body looked very familiar.

"Is that what I think it is?" Anders asked, pointing.

Lacroix smiled. "A tribute to my pet lion, Maahes. The head will be re-carved many times over the millennia, but you might know it by its modern name: the Sphinx."

Along the banks of the Nile, more men and women were tilling soil and planting crops.

Anders cupped his forehead. "Archaeologists have debated for decades about what triggered the Neolithic Revolution. I'd hoped one day to find the answer myself, but never in a million years did I dream it would have been us."

"A million?" Lacroix laughed. "Ten was more than enough."

"You must have other places like this," Riese said, transfixed.

"A few," Lacroix replied. "Some in Mesopotamia. The furthest we've gone is China. But our missions have not always been successful. The few tiny pockets of Neanderthals proved impossible to teach. One need not spend more than a few minutes observing them to understand they're an evolutionary dead end. Dumb, strong and easy to control, they have shown themselves

232

useful in other ways. Aren't those the most desirable qualities of any good farm animal?"

"Yes, we've seen your slave markets," Anders said with repugnance. "I'm surprised that a supposedly intelligent man such as yourself doesn't see the obvious contradiction."

Lacroix's eyebrows rose. "I see no contradiction."

"Your heightened sense of morality railed against Genesis' program of using human guinea pigs and yet you see nothing wrong with treating the Neanderthals like chattel."

Lacroix grew quiet. It was clear he didn't like being challenged, especially by those he was trying to impress.

The ship made a pass over what would one day become Cairo and as it did Lacroix finally spoke.

"You know already that Khan has launched several failed missions to unseat me. What I haven't told you was that many of those poor souls ended up as my prisoners. And believe me when I say I tried my best to reason with them. I'm a fair man. I'm sure you can see that."

The ship banked to the right and Lacroix grabbed hold of the leather loop hanging from the ceiling. "As such, each of them was given the same choice I'm giving you now. Be part of the next revolutionary leap forward for mankind or turn your back and share their fate."

233

Chapter 47

3 hours remaining

Once they returned to the island, Lacroix had Anders and Riese brought to separate quarters where they could shower, slip into some fresh clothing and come to a final decision on his proposal. He even offered to have a doctor check on Anders' chest, but Anders refused, saying that it stank worse than it hurt.

Anders' room was exquisite, with finished stone and finely crafted handmade furniture. Steam filled the bathroom as he washed away what felt like weeks of grime. There was even a fresh toothbrush which he used twice, back to back. He stood staring blankly into the mirror for a long time, contemplating what he should do and no less worried about the fate of his friends left behind in Xanbar. There was no doubt Lacroix was on the wrong side of history. But serious questions remained. What could he do about it and would Riese join him?

A new set of linen clothing was laid out on his bed. The tunic and slacks were earth-toned and very plain. There was a cultish quality to Lacroix's version of paradise that didn't sit well with Anders, and it wasn't simply the inordinate number of statues depicting Lacroix's majesty that made him feel this way.

Once dressed, he went across the hallway to Riese's room and knocked. She answered, fully dressed, her hair tied up in a towel. Judging by the expression on her face, he wondered if she was happy to see him.

"Can I come in?" he asked.

She shot a quick glance down both sides of the corridor. "Sure, but don't try anything."

"Give me some credit, would you," he said, stepping inside and closing the door behind him.

"You've got something heavy weighing you down. I can see it."

"Don't you? I mean, quite frankly, I'm one bad idea away from jumping on a Cutter and searching for those bodies in the mountains."

Riese bent over and shook the towel over her head before flipping her head back and letting her hair cascade over her shoulders. Anders felt warmth spread down his chest like a shot of good whiskey.

"You don't even know how to fly one of those things," she said.

"How hard could it be?"

She scoffed. "Probably harder than you think. Besides, where are you going to begin your search? And even if you find the spot, where are you gonna land to collect the bodies without risking contracting the virus yourself?"

"I was gonna worry about that when I got there."

"Why am I not surprised? I can almost guarantee those hikers are going to find an extra body frozen on that mountain. And I'll know it's you by the dumb look on your face."

"So what do you suggest, Riese? You're the virologist. Lacroix claims he destroyed the vaccine and time's quickly running out. I can't wait to hear your proposal."

"Nothing," she said flatly. Her cheeks were red from the shower.

"Nothing? So you're prepared to just let innocent people die? Hard to believe you once accused me of running from responsibility. Seems you're no better."

"That isn't fair."

Anders crossed the room and yanked open the curtains. Outside was a spectacular view of a waterfall surrounded by lush vegetation.

"You're not sure you wanna go home, are you?"

She fiddled with her old clothes, folding them neatly.

"That's it, isn't it?" he said accusingly. "You've found your little slice of heaven and now you wanna forget about the real world because it's not nearly as pretty." He peered through the window at a group of Neanderthals being forced to dig the foundation for a new building. Men hovered over them with whips shouting orders. "I can't believe that you of all people are being taken in by a glorified plantation owner with delusions of grandeur. Don't you see he's coming dangerously close to creating a paradox?"

She left the folded coverall alone. "What do you mean?"

"If he goes ahead and diverts the course of history far enough, the ripple effect might blink us all right out of existence."

"So he would never be sent back in the first place."

"Precisely. It's enough to give you a headache, but I know enough to say with confidence that the universe hates paradoxes. For all we know, it could very well tear the universe apart."

"Now you're just being dramatic."

"Am I?" Anders said. "The truth is we have people playing God and none of us have any idea what the consequences will be." He stopped and considered the strange expression forming on her face. "You're hiding something, aren't you?"

She looked away, but Anders could already see that he was right.

"After our conversation with Lacroix, I decided to take a closer look at the kid's blood sample in the sequencer," she said quietly. "I've never seen anything like it."

Anders held her by the shoulders. "What are you talking about?" he demanded. "And try to remember we didn't all graduate from Harvard Medical."

"The half-Neanderthal child, Aku," she replied, ignoring his dig. "Back in the native village, Khazanov had me take a sample of the kid's blood and run it through the DNA sequencer because he wanted to know the kid's genetic makeup."

Anders nodded. "Yes, and you saw that he was a hybrid. Great, I coulda told you the same just by looking at him."

She threw him a look. "And that was where I left things until Lacroix mentioned the Neanderthals demonstrated a natural resistance to the disease. Viruses need to mutate before they can jump from one species to another. It's the reason that in the past many of those pathogens we found frozen in the Siberian tundra didn't pose a threat to humans."

Anders wore the blank expression of a man in over his head.

237

"What I'm saying," she clarified, "is that Neanderthals have an HLA receptor labeled HLA-DRaDPb that provides them with a built-in immunity to Pyric Hemorrhagic Fever and other viruses in the same family. This probably explains why Genesis included them in the medical experiments. I'm almost certain the lab technicians were trying to find a way to insert that immunity into humans, but the species gap was causing problems."

"But the boy…" Anders began. "You're saying he's different?"

"His HLA receptors are a combination of human and Neanderthal."

"So you're saying Aku's blood holds a clue to creating a vaccine?" Anders said.

Riese and Anders locked eyes. "Not just a vaccine. I'm saying he may hold the cure." Then just as quickly her eyes fell away. "But he's somewhere in the jungle, probably wondering why we left him behind."

Anders had no interest in giving in to the pity party so soon. "I seem to remember him running off on his own, thank you very much."

She looked up at him. "So what now?"

He laid his hands on her shoulders and squeezed her gently. "Under the circumstances, we only have one option."

"Run away?"

"No. We need to kill Lacroix."

Chapter 48

Vacek, Stills and Halloway checked the magazines in their assault weapons before slapping them back into place. Three dead customs officials lay naked on the floor in the guard house by the pier. Stills was the tallest of the three and somehow got the shortest man's gray uniform.

"I look ridiculous," he complained, stretching his arms four inches past the end of the cuff. "Halloway, trade with me, will you?"

"Stop whining," Vacek barked. "Just keep your arms down and you'll be fine."

They headed toward the main research facility and the stasis chamber, which lay near the entrance to sublevel one. The intelligence had been quite specific, detailing the location as well as the number of guards they should expect to encounter. Since Lacroix had either cut the power or disassembled the machine, they weren't expecting much of a fight.

They entered the building and went down a set of emergency stairs toward the first basement level. A single guard stood before the transport pad entrance. The bored look on his face told them he was probably being punished with the dullest assignment on the island.

The guard straightened when he saw them approach.

"Please tell me you're here to relieve me," he said, chuckling.

Vacek tried to smile with only limited success. "Horrible gig, isn't it?"

"Tell me about it." The guard paused. "Wait a sec, aren't you guys from the customs depart—"

Vacek swung the butt of his rifle into the side of the man's face, dropping him to the ground in a heap. They entered the chamber, switching on the lights. Halloway dragged the young guard in by the collar and let him go. His head made a slapping sound as it smacked the ground.

"Don't leave him there," Vacek scolded the medic, setting the suitcase on the floor. "Stuff him in the closet."

Halloway did as he was told.

"How long will the repair take?" Vacek asked Stills, who was rolling up his sleeves and looking overwhelmed.

"Well, by the looks of things, he's removed the power couplings and severed the link to the gravity amplifiers. This might take a few hours."

"You have thirty minutes."

Halloway came out of the utility closet and struggled to push the door closed.

"Find Lacroix," Vacek told him. "And make sure he and anyone around him is good and dead before you leave."

"And what, if you don't mind my asking, are you gonna do?" Stills asked, opening a drawer and pulling out a wrench.

240

Vacek lifted the case and smiled. "I'm gonna collect a water sample."

•••

Anders and Riese were hurrying through an open square. Surrounding them were large imperial-style buildings, but the real showpiece was the fountain, featuring Neptune riding on six dolphins. Throngs of people were heading in a dozen different directions.

Riese pulled on his arm. "I'm with you about stopping Lacroix, but there's got to be another way."

"I've been wondering that myself, but for the life of me, I don't know what that is."

"Why don't you try reasoning with him?"

Anders scoffed at the idea. "Lacroix is one loose screw away from the nuthouse. He's hardly a man who can be talked down."

"You managed to convince me," she said, a light appearing in her eye.

"That's just my rugged masculinity, Riese."

"Oh, you conceited bastard."

A voice called Anders' name. He spun on his heel to find Binh and Jim heading toward them. Both men were dressed as locals. It seemed they'd managed to find passage to the island after all.

"Binh," Anders shouted with joy. He went to embrace his friend, but instead took a punch to the mouth. He blocked the next blow and grabbed Binh by the shoulders. Binh proceeded to fire an arsenal of expletives in his direction.

"I haven't understood a word he's been saying," Jim told them. "Although I can tell you for certain he's been really pissed off."

"We didn't abandon you, Binh," Anders tried to reassure him. "Lacroix's men kidnapped us." Binh was still wearing his watch. "I thought you traded this in?"

"Your little friend here's got some sticky fingers," Jim said, pretending to whisper.

Reluctantly, Binh handed Anders the watch, which he slid back over his wrist.

"Have you seen any sign of Erwin?" Anders asked.

Binh shook his head.

"I was never the guy's biggest fan," Anders admitted. "But I'd hoped we'd find him waiting for us here."

"We did see someone else," Jim said.

Binh explained that they'd seen Vacek and his men boarding a boat heading out of Xanbar. Worse, they'd seen him carrying the metal briefcase.

Anders bit his lip. The situation had just become infinitely more complicated.

"Maybe he tracked the case," Riese suggested.

Another scenario was just as likely. "Maybe he caught up with Erwin, who was persuaded to divulge its location." Anders had to think fast. "If Vacek triggers that bomb then it's game over for all of us."

Binh asked him about the vaccine.

"Khan lied," Riese told him. "Lacroix shut the bioresearch program down as soon as things got out of hand."

Anders glanced at his watch and then back to the others. "Find out where they're keeping that stasis chamber. Now that Vacek's got his bomb, there's no telling how long we have."

Binh shook his head.

Anders took off then and didn't get further than five feet before Riese called after him.

"What about you?"

"I'm gonna try to talk some sense into Lacroix."

"What if he doesn't listen?" Jim asked.

Anders' face twitched. "He will when I tell him what Vacek's got in store."

Chapter 49

1 hour remaining

Anders approached the pavilion, brushing through the crowd of locals and Genesis folk alike. He knew there were risks involved with going to Lacroix first rather than searching out Vacek on his own. But as head of the island, Lacroix had an entire security apparatus he could call on in order to find and apprehend the mercenary before he had a chance to arm and detonate the nuke.

Anders had a suspicion the other men in Vacek's unit knew nothing of the true purpose of his mission. If he could convince them of the merc leader's true intentions, there was a chance they might have a change of heart.

But first he needed to find Lacroix, a task he feared might not be as easy as it seemed. Anders had bet a man with his level of responsibility would be in his office, hard at work. It just so happened that his idea of an office was what most of us thought of as a temple.

But nevertheless, that was where Anders was headed, sprinting at top speed.

He reached the stone steps of the vast domed building and began working his way up. By the time he reached the top, his lungs burning in his chest, a series of loud pops echoed through the chamber. Ahead of him Lacroix slumped forward on his desk, shot by a man in a gray uniform. Nearby lay the prone body of his bearded security guard, Garcia.

The man with the gray uniform glanced up and fixed his weapon on Anders.

The chamber was wide open, which meant there was nowhere for Anders to run. He lifted his hands in the air.

"You're making a terrible mistake, Halloway," Anders said, taking a step back toward the stairs.

Halloway fired off a round, which struck the marble floor at Anders' feet. A small cloud of marble dust rose up.

"I missed that time on purpose," he said. "Take another step and next time I won't be so unlucky."

"Your boss has no intention of making it off this island."

Halloway was coming closer. "Says who? Stills is fixing the stasis pods as we speak."

"Maybe so, but he'll never get it done in time and Vacek knows that."

"How the hell do you know?"

Anders swallowed, trying to keep his eyes off the barrel of the assault rifle aimed at his head. "That case he's carrying, what did he say it was for?"

Halloway thought for a minute. "Water analyzer." The medic's eyes flickered as he said the words, as though even he could see his own stupidity.

"It's a suitcase nuke, Halloway, although I'm fairly certain you've already worked that out for yourself. He doesn't really work for Genesis. Never did. He's an assassin for a group called the Epsilon Brotherhood and he's here to make sure this island is sent to the ocean floor."

Halloway raised the rifle. "Prove it before I waste you the way I wasted this crazy bastard Lacroix."

Anders' arms were still in the air when he pointed to his left wrist. "His tattoo. Five rings in the form of a cross. It's the symbol for the Brotherhood."

The muzzle of the barrel lowered, only by an inch, but that was enough.

"You've seen it, haven't you?" Anders said.

Halloway nodded absently. "I asked him about it once and he told me to mind my own damn business."

"I need to know where he's planting the bomb," Anders said. Beads of sweat were streaming down his forehead and into his eyes. He blinked away the pain.

"The reservoir," Halloway said, distantly. "But we're already too late."

•••

By the time they reached Vacek he had armed the bomb and dropped the airtight case into the aquifer. His rifle was leaning against the concrete opening when Halloway ordered him to freeze.

"The hell are you doing?" Vacek said. He jabbed a finger in Anders's direction. "You're supposed to shoot him, not me."

"I don't know how, Chief," Halloway said. "But you're gonna have to jump in and turn that thing off."

Pedestrians passing by saw Halloway's drawn weapon and scattered, many of them screaming. They were in a narrow area between two buildings. A walking

246

path ran alongside the reservoir, lined on the left by a series of waist-high bushes. If they weren't careful, they might start a panic.

"Ten minutes from now, it won't matter anymore," Vacek said. "I'm ready to die for my convictions. Are you?"

Halloway ordered Vacek once again to stand down when a guard shouted at them from the balcony of a nearby mezzanine. Halloway's attention was gone for only a second, but that was all the time Vacek needed. He reached for his rifle and fired. One of the rounds struck Halloway and sent the medic sprawling to the ground.

Anders leapt for the bushes right as Vacek swung the barrel in his direction. He hit the pavement hard, skidding between two shrubs. That was when the guard opened fire, hitting Vacek once in the chest. He ducked behind the mouth of the well, his breath wheezing as though his lung had been punctured.

Fifteen feet away, Halloway lay unmoving. His weapon was on the ground between them. When Vacek raised himself up to fire on the guard, Anders rolled out from behind cover and grabbed the assault rifle. He'd never fired a gun before, but in that split second of panic, it didn't seem to matter.

Anders held down the trigger and the weapon kicked in his hands, jumping wildly as though he were holding the reins of a bucking bronco. Chunks of pavement around Vacek flew in the air. Vacek returned fire, forcing Anders to take cover behind a waist-high wall. Full auto clearly wasn't working. Adrenaline coursing through his veins, Anders searched the weapon and found a selector switch. He flicked it to single shot and popped up over the wall, right as Vacek was charging at him. Anders pulled the rifle into his shoulder and pressed the trigger five times in rapid succession.

247

The first four shots chewed up bits of dirt and concrete on either side of the mercenary leader. The final round hit him right above the eyes, snapping his head back.

People nearby shouted with terror while the guard on the mezzanine looked on with confusion. But before they had a chance to put the pieces together, Anders dropped the weapon, switching it for Vacek's as he ran off.

It was only after he'd skidded around the corner that he checked his watch. Time was compressed when bullets were thudding around you. Vacek had boasted that in ten minutes none of this would matter anymore. By the looks of it, they still had eight minutes before they were vaporized in the core of an artificial sun.

Chapter 50

Anders arrived at the stasis chamber and found Jim holding a rifle on Stills. On the walls, the lights from control panels glowed blood red.

Anders stopped to catch his breath. "I really wish I had more time to explain, but this whole place is about to go up like a Roman candle, compliments of your friend Vacek."

Stills looked at him strangely.

"Please tell me this thing is working," Anders said.

"We got enough juice for one trip, kemosabe," Stills told him. "I might be able to get it fired up if Rambo over here would put that gun down."

Anders pushed the barrel of Jim's weapon toward the floor.

"Came in and saw it sitting on the table," Jim said, shaking the rifle with pride. "Snatched it up before he could say a word."

Binh arrived with an armful of valuables.

"Are you crazy?" Anders shouted. "What is all this stuff?"

Binh explained it was from Lacroix's penthouse suite.

"I don't believe you." Anders checked his watch and saw they had seven minutes left.

"At least tell me you know where Riese is."

"She saw Aku arrive on the island right after you left," Jim said. "Kid was in chains, being led by the slave trader from the market."

"Crap," Anders said and bolted for the door. "If I'm not back in six minutes, go back without us."

They stared as he left.

Anders exited the building and ran for Gihon's marketplace. Anders guessed that was the most logical place for a slaver to go. Halfway there he found Riese in a heated argument with a man. She was telling him the child belonged to her and the argument wasn't going very well. The slave trader held Aku by one of his thin arms, shaking him about as the two shouted at one another. When Anders arrived, the trader saw his weapon and threw up both hands.

"I don't need your help, Anders," she insisted. "See, now he thinks you're going to shoot him."

Anders took one final look at the time—noting they had five minutes left.

"What does he want for the boy?" he asked.

"His English is not very good," Riese said. "Seven thousand Lax, whatever that is."

"We don't have time for this," Anders told her. "I couldn't stop Vacek before he armed the bomb. If we're not gone in the next few minutes, we'll become permanent residents."

"Yes, but we can't just leave Aku here to die. Give me the gun," she said, reaching for Anders' rifle.

The slave trader looked on with confusion.

250

"I'm not gonna let you shoot him," Anders said. He slung the weapon over his shoulder and removed his watch, handing it to the trader. "Worth at least ten thousand Lax," he lied. The trader inspected while the seconds ticked away. After a moment, he nodded and handed the boy over.

Families in tunics ran past them, carrying their belongings, heading for the port.

"The shootings have got people panicking," Anders said as he took Aku's hand and led them back toward the stasis chamber. "It's just as well given this place is about to get a makeover from the inside out. But we need to hurry. Stills had a look like he was itching to head back with or without us."

With every step, Anders counted down the seconds in his head. They reached the stasis room and he swung open the door. Riese rushed inside, but Anders hesitated. She skidded to a stop when she saw he wasn't following.

"What's wrong?"

Anders looked down at the boy, then back at her. Aku was still wearing the necklace with the items dearest to him—a lock of his mother's hair, one of her teeth and the Genesis patch Anders had given him. "What do you think will happen if we bring him back with us?"

"We'll find a cure," she replied, dread in her voice. "What are you getting at?"

"I know what'll happen. He'll be kept in a cage and turned into some kind of lab rat. We do that and we're telling Genesis that everything they did here was all right. Torturing and dissecting innocent people is fine if it saves lives. Is that really the kind of world we want to live in?"

"Anders, we don't have time for this."

"We may not, but we can't afford not to. Head to the transporter. I told them if I wasn't back to go ahead without me."

251

"Don't be a hero, please. I'm begging you." Her eyes more than her words were pleading with him.

He closed the door, Aku's hand held tightly in his own. Together they ran. He had less than three minutes and every second was going to count.

•••

Back in the stasis chamber, a clock on the wall registered a minute forty-five seconds and counting. There were twelve pods, one for each of them with a few to spare. Riese sealed her hatch shut and watched the clock tick down. The timer was set to engage the device as soon as the board reached zero. Already bolts of blue lightning were beginning to arc between the pods.

Anders wasn't going to make it. He'd had a last-minute crisis of conscience and now everything they'd fought so hard to achieve was gone. Assuming this contraption even worked, she would be shot back into the twenty-first century without a cure and, more importantly, without him.

The clock was down to the last twenty seconds when Anders finally came charging into the room. A blue halo began to form, changing the color of his skin as he struggled to open the pod and climb inside. Ten seconds left and he wasn't going to make it. He jabbed his legs in one at a time and then twisted his body. Three… two…

That was when the room began to shake. Anders yanked hard on the hatch as the room exploded and everything went black.

Chapter 51

Anders came awake staring into the distorted face of a lab technician. She hovered over him, enveloped in a hazmat suit, her voice hollow and distant. He searched around. A battery of technicians were attending to the others, among them Riese. He reached out and her fingers touched his before they were pulled apart and put on gurneys bound for *Excelsior*'s infirmary.

Each of them was wheeled into the same room, their beds separated by a thin curtain on a noisy track.

When the sedative he'd been given began to wear off, Anders swung his legs over the edge and planted them on the cold floor. A nurse making the rounds at the far end was also wearing a hazmat suit. He scampered over and pulled back Riese's curtain. Her head rested on the pillow. She turned to see him. A weak smile appeared on her lips.

"For some reason I thought the trip back would be the easier of the two." She glanced down at his bare feet and the medical robe he was wearing. "I was sure you weren't going to make it. Where did you go?"

"I put Aku on one of the ships leaving the island. They weren't hard to find. Seemed most of Gihon was looking for a way out. At least the lucky ones."

"He could have come back with us," Riese pleaded. "Come back with a cure."

"After leaving the slave trader I realized something."

Riese regarded him with a furrowed brow.

"We didn't need the boy."

"What do you mean?"

"I mean the cure. It was with us all along."

•••

The following day Anders met with Khan and Davenport at the stasis chamber, along with Riese, Binh, Jim and Stills. Already, technicians were busy dismantling the equipment that had made the journey to the past possible. When the scientists were satisfied Genesis was severing its link to the tenth millennium BCE, they headed for the conference room.

Once there, Khan was the first to inform them that in the days since they had left, the virus had spread to a sixth of the population, well over a billion people. Among the dead were Meadows and twenty percent of *Excelsior*'s crew.

"How long were we away?" Anders asked.

"Four days," Khan said. "Although on your end it might have felt like more."

"I'm guessing Gihon still hasn't come back online," Anders said.

Davenport shook his head. "Can you tell us what happened?"

"You lied," Riese said. "That's what happened."

254

Davenport feigned confusion.

"You can save the act," Jim said. "I told them what I knew and the rest they pieced together on their own."

Anders filled them in on Vacek's mission from the Epsilon Brotherhood and his role in destroying the island.

"We know you were responsible for creating the virus," Anders continued. "And we also know you intended to use Gihon as a kind of lifeboat to escape the mess you started. Lacroix may have been mad, but at least he told us the truth."

The room grew cold and quiet after that. Finally, Khan crossed his arms and said, "I want to address this cure you claim to have brought back. We've received your demands and are in the process of implementing them."

"Whatever it is you people need to travel through that portal," Anders said, "we don't just want it dismantled, we want it destroyed, along with a written assurance you'll never try to build it again. The past is the past and it ought to stay that way."

"Already done," Khan assured them, waving Davenport forward. Davenport slid a document and a pen across the table.

"If Gihon was accessed by going through the third doorway," Riese said, "what about the other two portals you mentioned when we first arrived?"

"We did tell you there were three portals," Davenport confirmed. "And we also made it perfectly clear that the first two didn't lead anywhere."

Satisfied, each of them read the papers before them and signed their name.

When they were done Riese produced her DNA sequencer and handed it to Davenport.

"What's this?" he asked, puzzled.

"Have your technicians analyze the first blood sample," Riese told him. "They'll find everything they need inside."

"And what about our pay?" Jim asked, causing Binh to perk up.

"Each of you will be given what was promised," Khan answered.

"As happy as I am to hear you've destroyed the portal," Anders said, "there is a missing man to deal with."

"Dr. Erwin," Davenport replied. "Stills has already informed us that unfortunately, he didn't make it."

"It was Vacek," Riese said. "Wasn't it?"

Stills nodded, without looking any of them in the eye.

The meeting adjourned shortly after that. Khan and Davenport shook each of their hands as they left.

Anders exited through the sliding doors with Binh close behind.

As they left, Binh produced a wallet and began leafing through its contents.

"The hell did you get that from?" Anders asked.

Binh regarded him with a wry grin and confessed.

"Go give Davenport back his wallet before I turn your klepto ass in."

Binh tried to object.

"How should I know? Tell him you found it on the floor."

Binh ran back as Riese passed him heading the other way.

"So what now, Dr. Anders?" she asked.

"Not sure. I suppose Binh and I will head back to the *Lady Luck* and keep digging around, now that we know we're on the right track."

"Who would have figured that Gihon would come to be known as Atlantis?" She spoke the words slowly,

256

thoughtfully. "I guess in a roundabout way you found it after all, didn't you?"

His lips curled into a grin. "I suppose you could say that."

"The history books will need to be rewritten, you know."

He laughed. "I wouldn't go that far. Besides, who'll believe me?"

"I will," she replied.

They were walking down the corridor now, arm in arm. "You ever given any thought to becoming an archaeologist?" he asked her as they turned the corner. "I think you'd be quite good at it."

Chapter 52

One Year Later

"You better see this," Sykes called out over the walkie.

Anders told them he'd be right there, and stepped into the cave, the cool air brushing against his cheek. They were fifty miles south of Algiers in the Tell Atlas Mountains. Ever since returning home from the tenth millennium BCE, he'd been overcome with an almost obsessive search for something he'd left behind. A guide rope led the way. Halogen lamps dug into the cave walls cast long eerie shadows as he descended.

More than once in the days and months following their return, thoughts of Gihon had entered his awareness. He'd worried for a long time that their mission into the past and Lacroix's tinkering had altered the course of history. Instead, he came to realize their actions had helped to make sense of questions that had been plaguing historians for decades—questions such as the cause of the Neolithic Revolution, the subsequent rise of cities and the myth of Atlantis, an advanced island nation sent to the bottom of the sea in the blink of an eye. Who could have imagined that by stepping into the past, men from the future had planted the seeds of their very own evolution? It was the sort of thing you couldn't contemplate for long or else the room would start to spin.

Brain busters aside, the world was still reeling from the loss of over a billion inhabitants. It didn't matter that the vaccine had been produced and disseminated in record time. The damage, in most cases, had already been done. But the human race, fortified by that sliver of Neanderthal DNA we each carried within us, was resilient. Even so, the recovery would take time.

This was an irony not lost on Anders as he descended into the cavernous chamber. Thousands of years ago, ancient peoples had lived and slept here. Today, remnants from their daily lives were still visible: stone tools, piles of bones and on the walls splendid artwork.

Riese and Binh stood waiting for him. Next to them was Rodriguez, Carter and Sykes.

"It's gorgeous, isn't it?" Riese said, swinging a beam of light across the ancient images.

Many of these cave drawings were part of a hunting ritual, depicting animals these early people had hoped to kill. Others showed thin figures in an assortment of activities, some dancing, some swimming.

Binh motioned to a section of wall that held their latest find, the very reason they had begun their search.

The handprint of a male was the first thing Anders saw, and beside that the rough image of an island with a

259

dark cloud rising above it. He glanced at Riese and she motioned with her eyes. There was more.

Below the island Anders spotted something faint. He moved closer in order to make out what it was. On a small section of the rock wall he spotted the swish of a crescent moon, in the center of which sat a double helix. Genesis' corporate symbol. It was as though someone had dipped the company's shoulder patch in paint and pressed it up against the smooth stone.

"Aku," he said. His fingers settled over the handprint, followed by his palm in a tender attempt to bridge the thousands of years between them. "He must have been a man when he did this."

"It was because of you that he lived," Riese said. "Maybe even had a family."

Anders studied the images, every possible emotion surging at once within him. "What do you suppose he meant by it all?"

Riese contemplated Anders' question for several seconds. Then at last: "I think he was saying thank you."

•••

The doors to *Excelsior*'s conference room swished open and the lab technician stood by the entryway, motioning to Mr. Khan.

Khan sighed, wondering why the highest-paid science types always seemed to be blessed with the most atrocious manners. He raised his index finger and held it there for the technician to see. Delegates from three of the largest nanotechnology firms were seated before him. Khan wasn't going to be made to look like a fool in front of them.

Khan smiled, motioning to Davenport, who was seated next to him. "Gentlemen, if you'll give me a moment."

He stood and stomped across the room to the noticeably nervous man in the lab coat.

"If you have something important to say I suggest you say it fast," Khan snapped.

"The second doorway," the technician replied. "The one we sent probes and then a man into."

"Yes, I remember perfectly well," Khan said, folding his arms. "Nothing we sent through survived."

The technician hesitated. "Well, that isn't entirely true."

Khan's eyes drilled holes into the man's skull. "What are you talking about?"

"A message finally came back, sir."

"A message?" Khan hung onto that last word, drawing it out.

"It was composed of short and long beeps," the tech told him.

"Morse code?"

The tech nodded.

"What did it say?"

The technician held up a quivering scrap of paper he'd pulled from the readout. "It was only one word."

Khan studied the message, the blood draining from his face.

It read...

H... E... L... P.

Thank you for reading
The Genesis Conspiracy!

Want to be notified of James D. Prescott's next
release?
Email me at jamesdprescottauthor@gmail.com and
I'll be happy to add you to my mailing list.

Real life versus fiction:

As fantastical as the idea for *The Genesis Conspiracy* may have been, much of what was included in the novel was based on fact. I've listed some of the larger ones here, although there are plenty of others I've left out.

Atlantis:
According to Plato, the advanced civilization of Atlantis was a real place situated on an island just past the Pillars of Hercules (Straits of Gibraltar). Although most archaeologists consider Plato's account more figurative than factual, others continue to search the depths of the world's oceans for clues to its final resting place.

The Neolithic Revolution:
Archaeologists continue to speculate why humans, after tens of thousands of years as hunter-gatherers, suddenly made the leap to an agrarian way of life starting around the tenth millennium BCE. Dozens of theories have been offered and still the debate rages on. In *The Genesis Conspiracy*, I set out to answer this question in a thought-provoking and entertaining way.

Neanderthal extinction and virus immunity:
Another subject which has long puzzled scholars. Initial theories posited Neanderthals were driven out after *Homo sapiens* moved into Europe. Other ideas have focused on the role of climate change and dwindling resources. Modern genetics has recently shown that, unpopular as the idea may be, our ancestors mated with Neanderthals. Each of our genetic codes is comprised of 1%-4% Neanderthal material. Among the several traits they possessed was an HLA receptor that gave them

immunity against a host of viruses native to the European environment in which they lived.

Pathogens dug up from the permafrost:
In 2014, scientists in Russia unearthed a 30,000-year-old virus from the melting Siberian permafrost. Although it posed no threat to humans, with the planet's melting ice, who's to say whether we'll be so lucky with the next one?

Ancient bodies trapped in glaciers:
In September of 1991, hikers in the Alps on the borders between Austria and Italy came upon a 5000-year-old body frozen in ice. Along with the find came a treasure trove of artifacts which helped to paint a vivid picture of life in the area during the third millennium BCE. The body came to be known as Otzi because of the area in which he was found. Scientist studying his body continue to make fascinating discoveries.

Sahara Climate:
The climate in the Sahara has shifted many times over the millennia. During the tenth millennium BCE (when the novel is set), the Sahara was marked by rivers, lakes and grasslands. The story shows the area as a jungle, a liberty I took, since it was a more interesting setting and didn't completely depart from the reality that the area would have been largely unrecognizable.

Printed in Great Britain
by Amazon